Death By Deceit

A Josiah Reynolds Mystery

Abigail Keam

Worker Bee Press

Published in the USA by

Worker Bee Press
P.O. Box 485
Nicholasville, KY 40340

Acknowledgements

Thanks to my editor, Penny Baker.

Artwork by Cricket Press
www.cricket-press.com

Book jacket by Peter Keam
Author's photograph by Peter Keam

By Abigail Keam

Josiah Reynolds Mysteries
Death By A HoneyBee I
Death By Drowning II
Death By Bridle III
Death By Bourbon IV
Death By Lotto V
Death By Chocolate VI
Death By Haunting VII
Death By Derby VIII
Death By Design IX
Death By Malice X
Death By Drama XI
Death By Stalking XII

The Mona Moon Mysteries
Murder Under A Blue Moon I
Murder Under A Blood Moon II
Murder Under A Bad Moon III

The Princess Maura Fantasy Series
Wall Of Doom I
Wall Of Peril II
Wall Of Glory III
Wall Of Conquest IV
Wall Of Victory V

Last Chance For Love Series
Last Chance Motel I
Gasping For Air II
The Siren's Call III
Hard Landing IV
The Mermaid's Carol V

1

Veritas Noble and I had just seen the classic *The Apartment* with Jack Lemon and Shirley MacLaine at the Kentucky Theater and were heading back to her car when she exclaimed, "Oh, Josiah. Someone has run into my Subaru Impreza!"

We both rushed and surveyed the damage to the back of her bumper which someone had severely dented.

"That's terrible," I said, looking around for cars whose color matched the paint marks scratched on the bumper. "Wait a minute, VeVe," I said, referring to my nickname for her, as Veritas was too much of a mouthful. "There's an envelope under the windshield wiper."

Veritas pulled a white envelope out from the wiper and tore it open. It contained a large wad of cash. "Josiah, there's a thousand dollars here," she said, incredulously.

"Read the note."

Pulling out a handwritten note she read—"*'I'm sorry. Hope this helps.'* Just when I thought the worst, I find this. Kind of restores my faith in humanity. My insurance has such a high deductible."

"Do you think the money will cover the cost of fixing the bumper?"

"It should be close enough. I feel so much better now."

"It was very nice to leave some money, but who walks around with a thousand bucks in his pocket?" I wondered out loud.

"I don't know and don't care. Let's go. I want to get home."

"Can you get my packages out of the trunk?"

"Yeah. Looks like the trunk wasn't affected," Veritas said, inserting her key and opening it.

How shall I put this? The trunk swung open. We both stared at its contents, gasped, and ran down the street screaming.

A dead man had been stuffed into Veritas' trunk.

2

Let me introduce myself. My name is Josiah Louise Reynolds. My grandmother named me after a righteous Hebrew king. I'm anything but. I'm not a king and definitely not righteous. I live on a farm near the Palisades in the Bluegrass overlooking the Kentucky River. I raise honey bees and make my living selling honey at the local farmers' market, boarding horses, and renting out my iconic home, the Butterfly, for events like wedding receptions.

I'm in my fifties, wear a hearing aid, walk with a slight limp, and in pain much of the time, although the pain has lessened. I am mannerly, housebroken, and presentable in public without embarrassing myself or others—most of the time.

That takes care of me.

As for Veritas, she is an old friend, and we had spent an enjoyable evening together until we opened the trunk of her car.

We ran screeching pell-mell, coming to a halt only

when I careened into a parked car. I grabbed hold of Veritas' jacket. "Stop, VeVe. I can't go on."

"I think I peed on myself," Veritas said, glumly.

"You're not the only one who needs to change her panties. Come on. Let's see about this."

"No."

"The man might need assistance."

"He looked dead to me, Josiah."

"Stay here, then. If someone is playing a gag, and that stiff jumps out at me, I'm gonna make sure he's dead."

I made my way back to the car parked behind the theater. The trunk was still open, and the street was eerily quiet as if nothing untoward had happened. Peering cautiously into the trunk, I sputtered, "Sir, are you all right?"

I inched closer still and poked him with a finger. The man's head lolled to where I could see his face. He was dead all right. His eyes stared up at me with that blank look that only the dead have. I should know since I've stumbled upon my share of lifeless bodies during the past few years.

Digging into my purse, I pulled out my phone and used its itty bitty light to get a better look inside the trunk. The unfortunate man was a white male with nice features who must have been handsome in life. He was thirtyish, wearing expensive blue jeans, posh tennis shoes, black tee shirt, and jacket. His hair had been cut recently, and his nails appeared to be professionally manicured. Rigor mortis had not set in yet, which meant the man had died within the last three hours. My concentration was broken by the clip-clop of Veritas' approaching steps.

"Is he?" Veritas asked.

"Sure looks like it."

"How did he die?"

"Don't know but there's a small blood pool underneath him. Better get the police, VeVe. I'll stay here with the body while you go."

"I'll be back in a jiffy," Veritas said, quickly walking to the police station only a block away.

I took the opportunity of her absence to rifle through the man's pockets and go through his wallet. I switched on my phone's camera, taking pictures of both the body, possessions, and the dented bumper before the police arrived. I even took a small paint sample from the scratching on the bumper and dropped it into an empty pill bottle in my purse. Seconds later, a squad car with two uniforms pulled up with Veritas riding in the back. I turned with a frightened, panicky look plastered on my face for the benefit of the male policemen who expected such scared looks from women after stuffing my phone in my pocket. Who am I to stand in the way of archaic prejudices?

A beat cop nudged me aside and felt for a pulse. "Yep, he's dead." He eyed us suspiciously. "Touch anything?"

"Why no, Officer," I lied. "Why would we do that?"

"Did you know him?"

Both Veritas and I shook our heads.

"Whose car is this?"

"Mine," Veritas said, her voice quaking a bit.

"We'll need you both to make a statement. This officer will show you to police headquarters."

"Don't bother. I know the way. Come on, VeVe. Let's get this over with."

"What a horrible evening," Veritas said, peering over her shoulder at the cop following us to the police station.

I couldn't have agreed more.

3

Norbet Drake walked into the interrogation room with a Styrofoam coffee cup in one hand and a file in the other. He glanced at me, shaking his head. "You are certainly a bad penny. How do you manage to keep any friends when bodies keep piling up around you? I would give you a wide berth."

"Nice to see you too, Norbet."

He sighed, "It's Detective Drake."

"We see each other so often, I thought we should be on a first name basis."

"It's rather like a revolving door for you and this police station. Okay, Josiah, let's hear your story this time."

"May I call you Norbet?"

"No."

"Then it's Mrs. Reynolds." I batted my eyelashes.

"Do you always act like this just to be difficult?"

"Hmm, yeah, I think I do."

Detective Drake cleared his throat. "Let's get on

with this." He clicked on the video recorder. "It is twenty-two hundred hours on Sunday——."

I interrupted. "He must have been shot."

Detective Drake looked up from his file. "What makes you say so?"

"Because you made VeVe and me take a GSR test. Who does that anymore? It's a rather outdated test, isn't it?"

"When you say VeVe, do you mean Veritas Noble?"

"Did you know Veritas was the Roman goddess of truth? VeVe, that's what I call her, is very much like her namesake. I don't think she's ever told a lie in her life. I don't think she even can. If VeVe says something, you can take it to the bank."

"For this interview, let's refer to VeVe as Veritas Noble."

"Okay, but let's get back to the gunshot residue test."

"Mrs. Reynolds, I was under the impression I am conducting this interview."

"Interview? See, that's the problem. I thought we were merely giving statements as witnesses to discovering a body. My being interviewed means you think I'm a suspect. Did you find gunshot residue on my hands?"

Detective Drake leaned back in his chair. "NO! We didn't."

"So, I'm not a suspect?"

"My mouth waters at the thought."

"Did you find a gun on me, VeVe, or in her car?"

"Privileged information."

I replied, "Which means no. Did you find a gun anywhere in or near the crime scene like a dumpster or a storm drain?"

Detective Drake crossed his arms while clenching his jaw muscles.

I said, "I think the perpetrator took his gun with him."

"What do you think happened?"

"I haven't a clue. You're the detective," I replied in my best helpless female tone of voice.

"Will we find your DNA on the victim's body?"

"You will. I touched him to see if there was a pulse."

"What about Veritas Noble?"

"After opening the trunk, she never got close to the body again."

"Why did Mrs. Noble open the trunk?"

"I asked her. We had been shopping before the movie, and I wanted to get my packages from the trunk since we were going home."

"Why not leave them in the trunk?"

"It would save VeVe getting out of the car again when she dropped me off at home."

"What did you do when you saw the body?"

"We both ran away. I believe I was screaming. I think VeVe was, too. I ran headlong into another car. A bruise has formed on my leg. Would you like to see it?"

Detective Drake ignored my suggestion to see the bruise.

It used to be when I teased a man about showing part of my anatomy, he jumped at the chance. Now, men acted as if a bee had stung them. It's tough getting old, girls.

Drake asked, "Did you know the suspect?"

"It was dark and the man's face was turned away," I replied, trying to stifle a yawn.

Drake checked the report in the file. "The man's face was facing up when the officer arrived."

"Yes, only because I checked for a pulse."

"Did Mrs. Noble know him?"

"You'll have to ask her."

"Why did you park behind the theater instead of Main Street?"

"We went to see a movie and all the parking spaces were taken on Main Street, so we parked in the back."

"Why not use the parking garage half a block over?"

"Women dislike using parking garages."

"Even if it is attached to a police station?"

"We parked only a block from the police station and look what happened right under your noses. A man was murdered and thrown into the trunk of a woman's car."

"Okay, I've had enough. We'll call you back in if we need something further."

"You will talk to my lawyer, Shaneika Mary Todd, if you need something further. I gave your men a statement. I complied with your GSR test. I'm done talking. See ya around, Norbet." I gave Detective Drake a big smile, relieved the police hadn't searched me. For if they had, they would have found gloves tucked in my pants' pocket. Otherwise, my prints would have been discovered all over that dead man.

I may be a snoop, but that is no reason to make the police think I'm a killer.

4

A loud knocking at the door woke me up. Since Baby, my English Mastiff, wasn't growling, it must be someone he knew, and he didn't know anyone I didn't know. I pushed off the cat sleeping on my chest, and tried avoiding stepping on other felines from the Kitty Kaboodle, the clowder of barn cats, which were Baby's pets and let in every night. Two were curled around Baby still sleeping. One was on my dressing table, knocking off lipstick tubes. Another was climbing up the draperies.

I hurried to the front door and opened it. "Morning, Charles," I said to Lady Elsmere's heir. He was also her butler and estate manager. In other words, he was the big cheese at the Big House. "What can I do for you?"

"Good morning, Josiah. Her Ladyship would like a word with you."

"Now?"

"Right now."

"You woke me up."

"Please don't make me go back without you."

Seeing Charles' distressed expression, I assumed Lady Elsmere, aka June Webster from Monkey's Eyebrow, Kentucky was on the warpath about something. Probably one of my peacocks had pooped on her patio again. "Give me a minute to get dressed."

"Please hurry."

"Can I at least brush my hair and maybe my teeth?"

"If you must."

"Gee, thanks. Come on in. Help yourself to the fridge while I dress."

"Thanks, Josiah."

"Know what it is about?"

"Rather not say."

"Is it serious? Should I call a lawyer?" I teased.

"Nothing like that. I'll wait in the car until you get ready."

"Okay, be out in a jiffy." I hurried to my room, brushed my teeth, splashed water on my face, and threw on some clothes. I stumbled over Baby who had moved from my bedside to the front of the bathroom door. Mastiffs like to lie in doorways. "Good golly, Baby. You trying to kill me or somethin'? If I die, who is going feed you?"

Baby raised his massive head, yawned, and replaced his drooping jowls upon his paws, seemingly unconcerned by my threat.

After finding some flip-flops under a chair, I hurried out to the Bentley waiting for me. Ooh, June sent the important car to fetch me. Must be serious.

We arrived at the Big House, and Charles dropped me off at the back entrance. "Yoo-hoo," I called, striding into a large kitchen.

At the kitchen table sat Bess, Charles' daughter and cook extraordinaire, Amelia, another daughter and June's caretaker, and finally, June, the great lady herself.

June held up a newspaper. "What's this, and you didn't even bother to tell me?"

I grabbed the paper from June and read the front page. There was a large article about Veritas and me finding the body.

"What is it with you and dead bodies? It's becoming a filthy habit."

I replied, "I know. I know. They seem to be piling up, don't they?"

"One or two dead people is one thing, but there's been over a dozen in the past few years. It's unseemly and people are starting to talk."

"Starting to? Tongues have been wagging ever since Brannon left me for that skank half his age."

Ignoring the reference to my late husband's mistress, Ellen Boudreaux, June asked, "Why was I kept out of the loop?"

"It just happened last night, June. I got home late and went to bed. I haven't had time to tell anyone, let alone you."

Bess said, "I made a chocolate mousse cake for tonight, but you can have a piece if you spill. We want the skinny from the horse's mouth."

I sat down. "Breakfast it is then. I'll take one of your bribes anytime, Bess."

Bess jumped up and served a huge piece of chocolate deliciousness along with a glass of milk. Now, that's what I call a good breakfast. Sugar and chocolate. Better than caffeine to get a body going.

Amelia said, "It says a young man was found in the trunk of Veritas Noble's car."

"True," I replied, taking a big bite out of the cake. "His name was Shelby Carpenter."

"The newspaper article said the police weren't releasing the name of the victim until the family was notified," Amelia said.

"I'm nothing if not resourceful, Bess. I have my ways." I wasn't about to admit that I had sifted through the man's wallet, even to Lady Elsmere and her peeps.

"Shelby Carpenter. Shelby Carpenter," Bess mused thoughtfully. "Wasn't that the name of a character played by Vincent Price in the movie *Laura*?"

"I didn't know you like old movies," I said.

"Who was the victim?" June asked, ignoring Bess.

"I looked him up on the Internet. He was a freelance reporter," I answered.

"What does that mean?" June asked before taking a sip of her coffee.

I replied, "I gather he investigated stories on his own and wrote about them on his blog. Sometimes a newspaper would pick an article up. His blog had over six hundred thousand followers."

"Impressive," Bess said. "Where was he based?"

"Washington, DC."

June asked, "So he wrote about politics."

"A lot of the time, but anything that interested him I guess."

"If he was an investigative reporter, what was he doing here?" Amelia asked.

I said, "Better yet, who didn't want him to nose around the Bluegrass and was willing to kill him over it? Heard anything through the grapevine, June? You always have sources who feed you information."

"Ah, fiddle de de. Nothing but the scuttlebutt on Ferrina Landau's party to show off her new necklace bought by her doddering old fool of a husband."

Bess mused, "Is Ferrina one of those made-up names for white girls?"

"Everything about the woman is made-up from her pumped-up lips to her reconstructed bum."

"Easy there, June. People might think you don't like her," I chided, smiling. I loved it when June brandished her claws. "I take it that you're going to her party."

"Oh, wouldn't miss it for the world," June answered.

"I didn't get an invitation," I said.

"We can remedy that. I'll take you as my plus one."

"Ellen Boudreaux is Ferrina's best friend. She'll be there."

June huffed, "All the more reason for you to show up looking fabulous."

"I can't, June. I don't have anything to wear. The police still have my Dior dress. Even if they gave it back, it's ruined."

"Don't you have a little black dress?"

"Yes, but I reserve it for funerals. I can't be seen gallivanting about wearing it at parties."

"Very well, then. You can choose one of my couture evening gowns. I'll even throw in some of my jewelry."

"To keep? You're the best." I just loved teasing June.

June blustered, "To borrow, you cheeky wench. And I want my dress back in the same condition as you took it and the same stones on my jewelry."

"Switch stones? Good lord. You must think I'm some international jewel thief."

At the mention of a jewel thief, June pursed her lips. "I wonder how Liam is doing? Does he think of me?"

Who is Liam, you ask? Liam was a thief posing as the valet for June's nephew, Anthony, who planned to steal and embezzle from June. To make a long story short, Anthony was thrown out of the Big House on his ear, but Liam was allowed to stay as Charles' under-butler. Charles loathed Liam, but June set out to reform Liam and eventually took him to her bed.

Yeah, I wince at the thought of those two together as well. The upshot was Liam did steal some fabulous gemstones, but not from June, and no one had seen him since. The scuttlebutt was that he sold the gems on the black market and was living like a king in Europe. Since the gems had been missing for decades, and the true owner, Bunny Witt, had been murdered, no one filed a police report on them. So they officially never existed. No crime had been committed. Liam was free as a bird.

June had been bereft ever since. She longed for her "girl toy."

"Didn't you date Ferrina's husband, King?" I said, changing the subject.

"I did for a very short time after my first husband had passed away. Oh, my word, King was tedious. I think one of the reasons I went to Europe was to flee him. He ended up marrying one of my good friends, and, of course, they divorced several years later. I can only imagine how my friend must have suffered from boredom. It was much later when King met Ferrina and married her. He must have been in his fifties then."

Amelia said, "Ferrina had a baby right quick, too."

"Babies are always an insurance policy for a woman in May-December marriages, especially if there is a prenup involved," June said.

"Yes. Babies. They certainly can upset the apple cart though," I mused, thinking about the documents Shelby Carpenter was carrying with him when he died—among other things.

"What does that mean?" Bess asked.

"Nothing. I think I'll go up and select a dress now."

"I mean it, Josiah. No rips. No tears. No stains or you'll pay to fix it."

"Yes, your majesty," I called over my shoulder, heading toward the elevator. I took it up to the second floor and entered June's glamorous bedroom with its metallic silver wallpaper with Chinese pink blossoms and a silver bedspread on her king bed. I entered June's massive closet, which was as big as my bedroom suite and began going through her evening gowns. The closet even had its own filtering system to keep dust off June's clothes.

June had grouped her gowns into eras. All the gowns purchased in the sixties were grouped together as well as those from the seventies, eighties, etc. You get the picture. I skipped looking at the seventies gowns. Nothing pretty came of the seventies, so I headed for the sixties era. Each gown was tagged with the date purchased, where June had worn it, and what jewelry accessorized it.

There was another reason I looked through the sixties gowns. June had shrunk with age, so her dresses had become more diminutive over time. I thought I had the best chance of finding a dress that would fit me from the sixties. I had shed quite a few pounds over several years, but I knew the gowns from the nineties were a lost cause even with my weight loss. As I went through the couture gowns, I hummed the theme song from *The Avengers.* What would Emma Peel wear?

Pulling out one gown after another, I almost despaired. I couldn't find a dress that would fit me nor something I liked. Apparently a lot of ugly dresses were made in the 1960s as well as the 1970s. Then I came across a little black number that reminded me of the dress Audrey Hepburn wore in the opening scene of *Breakfast At Tiffany's.* I pulled it out and looked in the full length mirror while holding the dress in front of me. It would do. Simple but elegant.

By that time Amelia had come upstairs and poked her head in the closet. "Need any help?"

"What do you think?" I held out the dress.

"Lady Elsmere hasn't worn that dress in decades. It goes well with your hair." She looked at the tag. "She last wore this dress for a New Year's Eve party in London. Just been gathering mothballs ever since. Glad to see you're going to take it out and give it a spin."

I looked back in the mirror, cocking my head from one side to another, trying to make up my mind. "Do you have any long black evening gloves to go with this?"

Amelia went over to a wall of drawers and rummaged through one. "These will do."

I put them on. "They're perfect, don't you think?"

Amelia nodded. "How are you going to wear your hair?"

"I was thinking an updo."

"Perfect for the era. What about jewelry?"

"Does June have a tiara comb?"

Amelia laughed. "You mean like the one Audrey Hepburn wore? Every white woman wants to look like Audrey Hepburn in *Breakfast At Tiffany's*. Are you going to a party or dressing up for Halloween?"

I grinned sheepishly and shrugged. "Guilty as charged."

Amelia patted my shoulder. "Let's see what we can find. June has a choker that I think would look splendid."

I spent the next hour trying on the dress with different pieces of June's jewelry and finally selected two pieces. The dress was very tight, so Amelia was going to let out the seams for me. We made a pact not to tell June about the alterations. June's good nature would only go so far, and altering her clothes did not fall under the rubric of "borrowing" a dress.

I left feeling lighter knowing my fairy godmother had come to my rescue and instead of cinders and soot, I could go to the ball with my head held high. Cinderella had nothing on me.

5

For the next several days, I helped Eunice, my business partner, prepare baby quiches and double-chocolate peanut butter brownies for a wedding reception. On the day before the event, the tables were already set up on the patio around the pool, and several fountains had been installed in the pool water, giving a festive spray accented by rotating colored lights to delight the guests.

The local florist came and installed pink and white centerpieces and matching floating bouquets in the pool, while the wedding planner set the tables with white china with gold-rimmed bands, Waterford stemware, and pink lace napkins. Eunice set out the chafing dishes and then we took pictures before covering the tables with clear plastic tarps. I can say with absolute honesty that the Butterfly looked stunning.

The wedding was set for eleven the next day at an old stone church nestled between two horse farms, and the reception was for one o'clock sharp. Eunice and I would return to the Butterfly around eight in the morning, finishing up with cooking honey-glazed salmon with bourbon sauce, potatoes au gratin, and asparagus. I was assigned to pull out trays of Jell-O and use cookie cutters to produce wobbly dinosaurs, Sasquatch and R2D2 figures. Eunice thought this task was so simple that even I couldn't screw it up.

It was late, and we both were exhausted. I locked the front door to the Butterfly, and Eunice and I went our separate ways for the night. She went home to Versailles, and I took my golf cart to Matt's bungalow where Baby waited for me.

In the morning, Malcolm, Charles' grandson, would come for my English Mastiff, Baby, and take him to the Big House when I rented out the Butterfly. The cars and noise upset Baby prompting him to *protect* our home. It was best that he stay with Bess to whom I usually gave fifty dollars to babysit my big pooch until the event was over.

As I arrived and unlocked the door to the bungalow, I could hear Baby thumping his thick tail against the wall, waiting for me. There's no joy like a dog greeting his human mommy. No matter how tired I was, Baby always made me feel better because he was genuinely glad to see me.

I opened the door expecting a wagging tail and a big tongue lick. Instead, Baby shot past me, ran down the few steps into the yard, and tinkled. I went inside and poured myself bourbon neat. With glass in hand, I went back outside and sat on the porch watching Baby sniff here and there before he plopped down by my chair, happy that I was with him. I rested my feet on him, and Baby sighed deeply, content he was not alone anymore.

Matt's house sat on a ridge, so I could see the gentle rolling hills of the Bluegrass give way to the foothills of the Appalachian Mountains miles away. We called those foothills the knobs around here.

I sipped on my drink grateful that the day was over. Glad to have some free time, I turned on my phone and studied the pictures of Shelby Carpenter I had surreptitiously taken. I was thinking Shelby had been standing by Veritas' car when he was pinned by someone with another car. Being unable to run, Carpenter was shot point blank and thrown into the trunk of the car, which popped open by the collision. That would mean Carpenter would have more extensive damage to his body than just a bullet hole. The impact would have caused major trauma.

How could such a thing have happened downtown without any witnesses? And how long would it have taken someone to ram Carpenter, get out of their car, shoot him, pull their car back, get out of the car again, pick up Carpenter, and then throw him into the trunk, close the trunk, get back in their car, and drive off?

It had to have been a man. A woman alone couldn't have lifted Carpenter and deposited him in the trunk.

Putting my drink aside, I stepped over Baby and went to my golf cart. Curious, Baby followed me. Seeing me get into the cart, Baby jumped in, too, thinking he was going on a ride. Timing myself, I re-created the sequence of events I believed to have taken place. I repeated the actions several times. The shortest time I could achieve was four minutes. However, I believed a strong male could have accomplished the murder in three minutes.

Hmm. I sat in the golf cart thinking. Someone must have really hated Shelby Carpenter. It was a vicious murder. The only good thing about it was that his demise must have been relatively quick. Carpenter hadn't suffered long, although a minute of this torture would have seemed like an eternity if Carpenter was conscious throughout. But there was another possible scenario. It could have played out that Carpenter had been forced into the trunk at gunpoint and then shot because I didn't see blood on either the pavement or the side of the car. I really needed to see the autopsy report.

Regardless, Carpenter had been followed. I would have bet my house on that. I doubt this murder was one of random opportunity. Robbery was not a motive. As a reporter, he must have discovered something someone didn't want others to know, but why leave those folded-up documents in Carpenter's pocket? Did the murderer not have time to search him? Did someone suddenly come along, and the murderer had to shut the trunk to hide his crime? Once the trunk was closed, the murderer could not get it open again. It was only the impact of his or her car that forced VeVe's trunk to pop open in the first place.

I shuddered.

Going back inside the bungalow, I fed Baby and changed his water. Then I took Baby's brush and gave him a nice rub down. Lastly, I sniffed his fur. "A bath is in your future, old boy. I smell the very faint odor of a skunk encounter, but it will have to wait for a couple of days. Until then, stay away from wild critters." Baby knew what the word *bath* meant, and the displeasure showed on his face.

Scratching and muffled meowing sounded at the front door. Baby pulled away from me, ambled over to the door, pawing at it while glancing back at me.

"Okay. Okay. I thought we could get by one night without your pets." I pushed Baby aside and opened the door. Five cats ran inside and quickly made themselves at home. How did the Kitty Kaboodle even know we were here?

Baby barked a few times as if to remind the cats that they were guests in Matt's home. Ignoring Baby, the cats immediately went into the kitchen prowling for some grub. After spooning out some tuna fish for the intruders, I took a leisurely hot shower. That was a plus about living alone. I never had to worry about using up all the hot water.

Afterward, I took my kidney medication, changed my pain patch, massaged my bad leg, made a salad, watched some silly TV, and fell asleep. Not exactly an exciting life, but then again, I was alive.

Not like Shelby Carpenter, who was on a cold slab in the coroner's office.

I'll take pain over death any day. That is—until the pain gets too bad.

6

The wedding reception went off without a hitch. I got to the Butterfly at seven and had started the prep work by the time Eunice showed up. By eleven, the help had arrived and took the plastic covers off the tables which still looked great. No pesky raccoons had investigated during the night and wrecked them.

By twelve everything was in the chafing dishes except for the asparagus. I turned the fountains on and gave everything a last minute look-see before I checked in with Eunice. By twelve-thirty, some early birds began to arrive.

It was time for me to disappear. Eunice shooed me away. She would handle the rest by herself with the staff she had hired. I would come back around three and help with the cleanup. I wished Eunice luck and fled like the house was on fire.

Heading back to Matt's bungalow, I was going to take a much needed nap without interruption. No big slobbery dog. No meowing menaces. No Eunice snapping orders at me. Just lovely peace and quiet.

Or so I thought.

7

I awoke to the sound of the front door's squeaky hinges as it opened. I wondered if one of the reception guests was barging in by mistake. I looked at my watch. It was 2:40 in the afternoon. I had to be up anyway.

Jumping out of bed, I put on my shoes and went into the living room ready to help some poor sop find the Butterfly only to discover Matt standing in the doorway, looking around. He was holding his little girl, Emmeline.

I stood dumbfounded.

"Hi," Matt said with a smile that lit up a room.

Emmeline squirmed, so Matt put her on the floor. She immediately crawled toward me.

I picked her up and kissed her chubby cheeks. "What are you doing here?" I asked her.

She tugged at my hair in response.

"Do you remember me?" I asked. "Do you remember your Auntie Jo?"

Emmeline pointed a finger at me before putting my

hair in her mouth.

I pulled my hair away from her grubby little hands.

"Surprised?" Matt asked.

"Quite. Are you here for a visit?"

He shook his head. "Meriah has relinquished custody for good and only has visitation rights now. She was diagnosed with bipolar disorder. She was misdiagnosed. It wasn't postpartum depression as we thought."

"Really?"

"Yep. She's writing a new mystery and getting her life back on track. We had long talks about it, and she thinks I'm the more stable of the two of us, so I should have Emmeline."

"Uh huh. I believe she said that when Emmeline was born."

"A baby is more than she could cope with."

I put Emmeline down. "You don't say."

"So I've come home."

"For how long?'

"For good." Matt looked quizzically at me. "Aren't you glad to see me, Jo?"

I went over and hugged him. "Of course, I am. Just surprised, that's all."

"Why are you here?"

"The Butterfly is rented out for a reception. I slept here last night."

With a concerned look on his face, Matt looked around. "Where's Baby?"

"He's with Bess at the moment." I saw a car on the gravel driveway head towards Tates Creek Road. "Oh, my gosh, I'm late. I'm supposed to be helping Eunice at the moment. Honey, we'll have to talk later."

As I rushed past him, I gave him a quick peck on the cheek. Hurrying to my golf cart, I spied Matt follow me out onto the porch and watched me hightail it to the Butterfly. He looked confused.

I was confused myself because I really wasn't thrilled to see Matt. My lukewarm reception was indicative of my bewildered state. I couldn't help but wonder if his coming back to Kentucky was a mistake.

Here's the rundown on the past three years of Matt's life. Matt was my best friend who had a tempestuous relationship with Meriah Caldwell, the famous mystery writer. At their wedding, Lacey Bridges shot Doreen Doris Mayfield DeWitt in the head and then turned the gun on herself. Needless to say, the wedding did not continue.

Matt called their relationship off later, but when he was shot by Fred O'Nan (my stalker) during an attempt to murder me, Meriah packed up the seriously injured Matt and flew him to Los Angeles to recuperate. During his stay, Meriah gave birth to their daughter, Emmeline, and flipped out. Seemed like she suffered from postpartum depression—or so we thought.

Matt brought Emmeline home to Kentucky after he had regained his health, and everything was hunky dory until Meriah decided she wanted custody of Emmeline after all. She sued and won.

So Matt relocated to California to be near his daughter. Now Meriah had been diagnosed with bipolar disorder and wants Matt to have custody—again. It's been one crisis after another regarding their child, Emmeline, and quite frankly, I was worn out. Those two were constantly going back and forth, back and forth. It was exhausting.

I love Matt but I needed a long break from his roller coaster life. I hope this last custody agreement with Meriah was final. I was just getting too old for this crap.

8

I helped Eunice with the cleanup and took the trash and recyclables up to the main road for the garbage truck. When I returned, Eunice was waiting for me with a fat check and my half of the leftovers. Did I really need eighteen chocolate cupcakes decorated with white buttercream magnolias? No, but I'll eat them just the same as well as the leftover salmon and Jell-O R2D2s.

Thinking of my less than stellar behavior toward Matt, I made a welcome basket of cupcakes, salmon, Jell-O, pasta salad, wild rice, cold asparagus, and rolls.

While I was being tormented by O'Nan, Matt had stayed with me every step of the way, even when I begged him to live in town for his own safety. I knew he'd get caught in the crossfire sooner or later, but Matt refused to listen and stayed by my side until he was shot. In other words, he took a bullet for me.

I was ashamed of my behavior. Matt was going through a rough patch so I needed to be there for him.

On my way out the door, I grabbed a couple bottles of wine to go with dinner. Maybe if I got Matt tipsy enough, he wouldn't remember my shabby welcome earlier in the day.

One can only hope.

9

Matt was thrilled to receive the left-over goodies from the reception and acted as if my boorish behavior had never happened. Why can't I be that gracious?

We had a nice dinner and then I returned home to collapse in my bed and sink into a deep sleep which I needed. I was still in bed when I heard the front door open the next morning. What is it with people popping in on me?

Since I wasn't expecting anyone, I sat up immediately. Baby lazily got up from his bed and padded into the great room. It must be someone he knew since Baby wasn't growling.

Only four people had keys to my house—Lady Elsmere, Eunice Todd, Asa, my daughter, and my gentleman friend, Hunter. I had given him a key a few months back in a moment of weakness and even then wondered if I was going to regret my decision. I put on a robe and while doing so heard Hunter's voice talking to Baby. Yep, most definitely regretted my decision.

The deal was for him to call before coming over.

I washed my face, brushed my teeth, and combed my hair. In an attempt to look somewhat groomed I put on some lipstick. My eyes looked blah in the mirror. Ah, what the heck. I put on mascara, too. I peered at my reflection. Satisfied that I looked somewhat human I went into the great room.

"Something smells good," I said.

"I'm making eggs-in-a-basket and pancakes," Hunter said cheerfully, flipping over a half dozen flapjacks.

I glanced over at my Nakashima table. "And you've already set the table. How nice."

"I know you had a big day yesterday and wanted to treat you. How did the reception go?"

"It went well. It was our biggest gig to date."

"I know you were worried that you and Eunice might not be able to pull it off."

I sat across from Hunter at the island and watched him cook. He poured a cup of coffee and set it down before me. "Eunice handled all the heavy lifting. Everything went like clockwork, and I got a nice big check to deposit on Monday."

"You know you can deposit the check with your phone now."

"Like I would trust that. Nope. I'll go into town on Monday and deposit the check in person like a grownup should."

Hunter grinned. "You're a throwback."

"There are certain things I don't trust—like a gentleman friend driving forty-five minutes to make a surprise breakfast for his lady friend."

"My lady love," Hunter corrected.

"Uh huh," I said suspiciously.

"Come on. Follow me." Hunter carried platters of food over to the table. Coffee and orange juice were already on the table.

I became alarmed. "It's not an anniversary or something, is it? Your birthday?" I never could remember that stuff.

"Don't worry. It's nothing like that, but I do have a motive."

"I knew it," I said, sitting down. "Well, I'm not going to complain as everything looks delicious." I poured syrup on my pancakes. "You want to tell me why you are bribing me?"

"I've been assigned to the Shelby Carpenter case."

I stopped eating. "How can you be impartial? You know one of the witnesses—me."

"I told Detective Drake that. He says everyone knows everyone else in this town. Besides, there was no one else. Everyone was tied up."

"I don't understand. Why call in a forensic psychiatrist?"

"This Shelby Carpenter was a person of note. Other bloggers are already posting about his death and conspiracy theories are hitting the internet."

"So Norbet wants this case cleared up fast."

"Nice and tidy with a bow. That's why I was called in."

"Hmm." I began to sweat. If the police knew I had taken photos of the contents of Carpenter's pockets, I could be in serious trouble. I had signed a statement that I had not touched the body except to see if Carpenter was dead. If they found out I had rifled through his pockets and took photographs, I could go to jail—and I mean some serious jail time. I had to get those photos off my phone! And I had to be careful with Hunter. If he suspected I had lied, he wouldn't stop until he ferreted it out of me.

I smiled at him. "So you are here to interrogate me?"

Hunter took a sip of his orange juice. "To interview you."

"I see."

"Anything wrong? You look a might peaked."

"No. No. This is certainly nicer than being dragged down to police headquarters."

Hunter cocked his head and studied me.

I lowered my eyes and cut into my eggs-in-a-basket which is basically a piece of fried bread with an egg in the middle. I decided to change the subject. "Matt's back in town."

"Yes, I know. He was out in his yard with Emmeline. I stopped and talked with him for a few moments."

"And?"

"What do you want me to say? I'm not happy about it. I wish he had stayed in California."

"Franklin will have to be told."

"He's in New York for a few days to see some shows. I'll tell him when he gets back."

"How do you think he'll take it?" I asked.

"If Franklin takes my advice, he'll give Mathew Garth a wide berth."

"I think Matt has changed."

"You've said that before. The guy's a narcissist. He's a user."

"He's always been good to me."

Hunter seemed irritated. "Let's talk about something else, shall we?"

"Of course. Thank you for making breakfast. I would have heated up some leftover salmon and stale rolls."

Appeased, Hunter smiled. "After my interview with you, let's go for a swim. I brought my trunks."

I grinned. "Why bother with trunks?"

"Why indeed," Hunter said.

We clinked our coffee cups together and settled into a comfortable patois.

I have to say it was nice having breakfast with someone. Very nice.

10

Hunter conducted his official interview with me. It took over ninety minutes but I zigged and zagged the trickier questions. Yes, I lied. I told him I only touched the body to see if Carpenter was dead. Did I feel guilty? Uh, no.

I have a very strong distrust of authority figures, especially cops. I realize they have difficult jobs. I realize policemen are underpaid and underappreciated, but you've got to look at it from my perspective. I was almost killed by a renegade cop who used his position of authority to make my life miserable. He shot Matt. He shot Franklin. He shot Baby. He pulled me off a cliff and then tried to kill me again by throwing me off the Cumberland Falls.

Then there was the character assassination Asa experience. She blew the whistle on corruption in the Secret Service and got pilloried for it. Doing the right thing had cost Asa's career in government service and her marriage. She got back on her feet, but it turned something deep inside her that was dark and sinister.

Yeah, I lied my fanny off. Here's how it went.

"Why were you downtown?"

"Veritas Noble and I went to see a movie at the Kentucky Theater."

"What movie did you see?"

"*The Apartment* with Jack Lemmon and Shirley MacLaine."

"What did you do after the movie was finished?"

"Walked back to Veritas' car."

"Where was it parked?"

"In the parking lot behind the theater."

"Did you see anyone?"

"Just people who had also attended the movie and had parked there."

"What happened?"

"Veritas noticed her car had been hit."

"Where?"

"The right rear bumper and side."

"What did the two of you do?"

"We both examined the damage. Veritas was very upset. Then she discovered the envelope on her windshield."

"Tell me about that."

"It was a plain utilitarian white envelope with a thousand dollars in cash as well as a note."

"Tell me about the bills."

"There were about four one-hundred dollar bills

and the rest were fifties and twenties."

"Anything else?"

"Well, we didn't write down the serial numbers of the bills if that's what you're after."

"Who do you think left the money?"

"Shelby Carpenter."

"Why do you think that, Jo?"

"I think he hit VeVe's car. Left money with the note on her windshield."

"That's awful risky. Anyone could have come by and stolen the money. Why not leave a card with a phone number."

"Because he didn't want anyone to know he was in town. He was an honest man, felt bad about the accident, and left the money to cover the damage."

Hunter typed furiously on his laptop.

"So he must have had his own car. Perhaps a rental. Has it been found yet?" I wondered.

"I'm asking the questions here."

"We know he wasn't riding in a cab."

Hunter looked up from his laptop. "Why do you think that?"

"Because a cabbie would have notified his insurance company if he had hit a car. They wouldn't leave cash. No. No. It had to be Carpenter's vehicle which hit VeVe's car."

"And someone just came along and plugged him?" Hunter made a face.

"Well, what's your theory?"

"You know I can't discuss details with you."

I mugged a face, too. "Party pooper."

"Let's get this interview back on track."

"Okay."

"Veritas Noble found the money. Then what did she do?"

"She put it in her purse, much happier I might add. Then I asked her to get my packages out of the trunk."

Hunter asked, "She opened the trunk?"

"Yes, that's when we discovered a man lying in the trunk, and we both took off screaming down the street."

"Then what happened?"

"I ran into a parked car, and Veritas ran out of steam."

"Anybody come to your assistance?"

"No."

"I thought you said there were other people getting into their cars."

"By that time everyone had left, and we were alone."

"What did you do then?"

"Veritas and I tiptoed back and looked into the trunk."

"Did either of you touch the body?"

"I did."

"Why?"

I sighed. "To see if the guy was alive or dead."

"Did Veritas Noble touch the body?"

"VeVe touch a stiff? Are you kidding?"

"Yes or no, please?"

"Nope."

"What happened then?"

"I've been all over this with the police."

"Come on, Josiah. You know how this game is played. Answer the question, please."

"I sent Veritas to the police station a block over, and I stayed with the body."

"Did you touch the body while she was away?"

"No." I did my best to maintain a poker face but I felt my nose grow longer.

"Are you sure?"

"Why do you keep asking if I touched the body again?"

"Because I know you."

"Nice." I thought for a moment. "When did the coroner say Carpenter died?"

"You know I can't discuss details of the investigation with you."

"What hotel was he staying in? How many days had he been here? Who was he talking with?"

"I'm conducting this interview. Now stay with me on this."

"If you won't tell me, I'll just ask Lady Elsmere. She knows everything that happens in the Bluegrass. She has sources the FBI would salivate over."

"You go do that. If she knows anything, let me know. I may have to ramble up to the Big House and interview her. Now I have just a few more questions. "Did you know Shelby Carpenter?"

"No."

"Had you ever read his blog before?"

"Never heard of him before I discovered him dead."

"Did you or anyone you know have any contact with Shelby Carpenter before his death?"

"I can only speak for myself. I didn't know him. Had never seen him before. Never knew he inhabited the planet."

"Did Veritas Noble ever speak of knowing Shelby Carpenter?"

"I hope you're not grilling VeVe like this. You'll cause her to have a nervous breakdown."

"I'll take that as a no. How did you come into contact with Shelby Carpenter?"

"I felt for a pulse on his neck."

"Did you move the body?"

"Yes. I had to pull him around a bit to get to the right spot on the neck. I think his head rolled to the side a little."

"Did you touch anything else?"

"Maybe his shirt."

"Was he still warm?"

"For God's sake, Hunter! What a question to ask?"

Hunter gave me one of his looks.

"Let's put it this way. He was room temperature."

"Meaning?"

"He had been in a hot trunk. That's all I'm going to say about it."

"When you touched Carpenter, did you go through his pockets or wallet?"

"No. That would be disturbing a crime scene." I did my best to look indignant and leaned forward. "If it looked like someone went through his pockets, it proves my theory."

Hunter sighed. "What's your theory again?"

"I think Carpenter was in town to investigate a story, and someone didn't like him snooping around."

"Why do you think he was behind the Kentucky Theater?"

"Could have been meeting someone, or perhaps he just wanted to take in a movie and relax."

Hunter shook his head. "The police think it was a robbery—a simple crime of opportunity."

I leaned back in my chair. "Come now, Hunter. You know that's bogus."

"Enlighten me, Josiah."

I started to reply but stopped. Was Hunter setting a trap for me? If I said I knew for a fact that Carpenter's wallet and other documents were still on the body, I would be confessing that I searched the body. So I said, "Just a hunch."

Hunter gave me a queer look.

Dripping with sarcasm, I said, "A robber just happened to be along and remembering his Latin teacher saying 'carpe diem' and seized the day by robbing Carpenter, throwing him into the trunk of a car which Carpenter just happened to hit, and then drove Carpenter's car away? There are no hotels near that area, so Carpenter wasn't walking. He had to have a car. Give me a break, Hunter."

"Stranger things have happened."

"Then why didn't this mysterious robber take the thousand dollars from VeVe's windshield? He must have seen Carpenter take the money and put it on her window. Tell me, Hunter. Why was the money left on VeVe's car if this was a robbery?"

Hunter shrugged and continued typing on his laptop. "You're assuming Carpenter put the money on Mrs. Noble's car."

"There's no other explanation that makes sense." I tapped the table. "No, Hunter. Carpenter was followed, and the opportunity for murder showed itself. You need to find out what happened to Carpenter's car. Then follow the story he was working on, and you'll find the identity of the murderer. Just follow the story."

I watched Hunter type some more, giving him a long, hard look. Was Norbet Drake suspicious of my official statement? Did he send Hunter to trip me up? It was terrible being wary of one's own boyfriend. But then—that's me.

11

Fortunately, Hunter had to interview VeVe, so I got him out of the house. I watched Hunter pull out of my driveway, seriously regretting that I had given him a key. As soon as I lost sight of his car, I made a beeline to my office where I downloaded the Carpenter pictures on a thumb drive and printed out copies.

Taking the copies and bourbon neat, (yes, it was mid-morning and yes, I was drinking bourbon) I went out onto the patio. It was the first opportunity I had since the man's death to examine the papers he had stuffed in his pants pockets.

The first document was a twenty-seven-year-old Miami arrest record of a young girl by the name of Susan Dorsch aka Lolita aka Babydoll aka Smacktoy. It seemed Ms. "Smacktoy" had a long arrest record for prostitution beginning at the age of fourteen, and her last charge was for drug smuggling. The final entry noted the charges for prostitution were dropped, and she was put on shock probation for drug possession.

This told me that Susan had made a plea deal with the District Attorney. She probably gave up names and agreed to testify in court.

I looked at the picture on the arrest record and felt depressed. Susan was young when it was taken. Maybe seventeen. No more than nineteen at the most. She looked thin and ill. Dark circles under her eyes created a haunted look. This young girl had seen too much at too early an age and it showed. Dyed blonde hair created an unkempt halo. She kept it out of her face with pink children's hair barrettes in the shape of kittens. I took a deep breath, noticing the barrettes. Hence the assumed identities. It made me sick to think of that girl's life.

What had happened to force a young teenager into a life of drugs and prostitution? "You poor, poor little wren," I murmured, running my fingers over her picture as if that would provide some sort of comfort. Putting the arrest record down, I typed the name of Susan Dorsch into my laptop. Several Susan Dorschs popped up, but none of them looked like Carpenter's Susan Dorsch. I even got on Facebook and typed in the name. Again, several Susan Dorschs popped up. I vetted each one, but no one matched my Susan Dorsch in either looks or background. One was a grandma, another was an elementary school teacher, and the third candidate was an attorney in Kansas City.

I took a sip of my bourbon.

It was possible that Carpenter's Susan Dorsch was dead, or she had changed her name. I quickly did the math in my head. Let's say Susan was seventeen at the time of her last arrest. Add twenty-seven years. That would make Susan in her mid-to-late forties, give or take a few years. I brought the arrest record up close to my face and really studied the picture, imagining a few crow's feet around the eyes and a slacking jowl line. I had to admit Susan looked vaguely familiar but I couldn't place her.

I put the arrest record down since it was highly unlikely my path would have crossed with a lady-of-the-evening from Miami. Still, she looked familiar.

Of course, Kentucky has its own famous ladies of ill repute. Namely Bell Breezing in Lexington who was the model for the character Belle Watling in *Gone With The Wind*. Belle got her start in Mary Todd Lincoln's home on Lexington's Main Street, which had been sold and converted into a cathouse.

Prostitution was so bad in Lexington, Kentucky in the early years of the twentieth century that in 1915 a committee was founded to study the problem, and *experts* from the American Social Hygiene Association were brought in. Their findings astonished Lexington's fine churchgoing citizens. Lexington and surrounding areas had 55 houses of prostitution and 344 citizens working as prostitutes. They compared this to Richmond, Virginia, which had 54 houses of prostitution and 389 prostitutes.

So what?

Well, Richmond had a population of 150,000 while Lexington had only a population of 40,000. Lexington had the same number of whorehouses as a city four times its size. The elegant and educated "Athens of the West" had become the "Sin City" of its age.

There was also the infamous Pauline Tabor in Bowling Green who put a milk can on her porch to signify business was open. She wrote a best-selling autobiography—*Pauline's: Memoirs Of A Happy Hooker.* She claimed she entertained many nationally prominent men high in government and church. Pauline didn't give out names, but enough clues that one could guess. Apparently, the oldest profession had a long and prosperous history in Kentucky.

I picked up another document. It was a Wall Street Journal article on insider trading. Boorrrring! I read another. It was a Washington Post article on several men being vetted as ambassador to Great Britain, and one of them was King. Bingo! Something close to home.

Was Shelby Carpenter investigating King Landau? For what reason I wondered? The man was retired and had Parkinson's disease. Just standing still the man shook more than a windmill during a tornado. Any dirt Carpenter could find on King would be old news. Unless Carpenter discovered that King Landau had committed murder, the statute of limitations would have expired on any crime. Who would care about insider trading at this point? Not I.

I spent the next couple of hours nursing my bourbon and reading Carpenter's blog, which had won several blogging and journalism awards. Papers like the New York Times, the Boston Globe, the LA Times, Wall Street Journal, and the Louisville Courier Journal picked up his articles.

Carpenter wrote about whatever took his fancy. His politics were a little to the left of mine, but it was certain that Carpenter was a man wanting to make the world a better place. His writing came across as precise, truthful, and inspired no matter what the subject matter. Carpenter had been a good reporter. His blog would be missed. The world needs people who told the truth, no matter how unpopular the message. Shelby Carpenter was one of those brave souls.

I felt a little peeved at whoever silenced his voice. Taking a last sip of my drink, I called for Baby who lumbered toward me from a shade tree where he had been taking a nap. Most of the day was shot. I'd take Baby for a walk, check on my honey bees, have a swim, take a nap, and then get up to pay my bills.

Whoopee! Don't I live a life of excitement!

12

The day of the Ferrina Landau's party had arrived. I had my nails and toes done, eyebrows waxed, and nasty hairs plucked from my chin. I even went to the extreme—I shaved my legs. Now that was going above and beyond!

Looking outside, I noticed it was getting dark. I put the finishing touch on my updo and looked in the mirror. I wasn't Audrey Hepburn pretty, but I would pass. At least for a couple of hours until my hair strayed from its pins and drooped, my lipstick wore off, I dropped food on my dress, or broke a heel on my shoes. That's how it was with me.

The doorbell rang. It must be Charles picking me up. I kissed Baby goodbye and admonished him to be a good boy while I was gone. I didn't bother with the cats. Those were Baby's pets—not mine. Grabbing my wrap, I hurried out the door where Charles stood by the Bentley. I felt like Cinderella entering my carriage and climbed in the back seat with Lady Elsmere.

"Good evening," I said.

June gave me the once over. "Nice selection," she said, approvingly.

"And you thought I was going to embarrass you."

"I do wonder about your taste in clothes sometimes."

"I have very good taste." Leaning over, I patted Charles' wife on the shoulder. She was sitting in the front seat. "Hello, Mrs. Dupuy."

"Good evening, Josiah. You look gussied up."

I grinned. "Don't I though."

Charles got in the driver's seat. "Everyone buckled up?"

"Charles, why don't you hire a chauffeur so you don't have to tote June all around town?" I asked.

June shot me a look of disgust. "You're always trying to stir up things."

Charles pulled out of the driveway. "I learn about the county's business driving *Miss Daisy* here."

June pulled her wrap tighter and harrumphed.

"Besides, who do you think supplies Her Ladyship with some of the gossip tidbits?"

"You?"

"While I'm waiting I talk to the staff. I know most of them from church and organizations I belong to. They love to shoot the breeze, especially if I have some of Lady Elsmere's special chocolates from Switzerland or a small bottle of bourbon."

"You use bribery."

"I sure do, Josiah." Charles looked in the rearview mirror. "Besides, I like to get away from the farm. Driving relaxes me."

"Who am I to challenge a system that works?"

June sniffed, "Charles is not working tonight. He and Mrs. Dupuy are guests."

"What charity is this for again?" I asked.

June answered, "It's to raise money to save our retired Thoroughbreds. Most owners just discard them after their racing or breeding career is over."

"That's a thing I hate about the racing business." I thought for a moment since I had rescued two abandoned racehorses which were eating me out of house and home. "It would seem the better course of action would be to make a law requiring owners to provide for a horse's retirement."

June said, "There are going to be some state senators there. Maybe you can chat them up."

It was my turn to harrumph. "Kentucky has one of the worst reputations for animal cruelty in the nation. If our lawmakers won't fund animal shelters, give out jail sentences to those who hurt animals, or stop the cock and dog fighting, I doubt whispering in their ears while sipping on champagne at a party is going to have the desired effect that you want."

"The FBI is starting a national database on those convicted of animal abuse to predict violent behavior.

Sooner or later, Kentucky is going to have to catch up with the rest of the nation on this issue," June said.

"I'll do my part," I said, "but horse owners are loath to spend money on a horse that's not bringing in the moola."

"Charles has a plan," Mrs. Dupuy said.

"Oh, really. What is it?" I asked.

"Charles is going to make subtle hints that I'll financially back any candidate who will push through any animal abuse laws."

I laughed. "Bribery has a long and healthy history in Kentucky politics. Good luck to you, Charles."

"I learned from the best," Charles said, winking at Lady Elsmere in the rearview mirror.

I looked out the car window. It was starting to drizzle. June and Charles may have an altruistic reason for going to this party, but I was going for another reason.

I was going to poke around.

13

I followed Lady Elsmere into the nineteen-thousand square foot monstrosity of a house that only the nouveau rich would build, and I felt smugly superior looking at the sterile, unimaginative but expensive furniture that every high-end hotel had in its lobby. It shouted second-rate decorator. Even the art was expensive but mundane, and uninspired. Art was something I knew about, having previously been an art history professor.

Some color caught my eye though and I gravitated toward it. It was a Hisel painting. Finally, a painting of note. I had never seen this particular work of Ms. Hisel's and was studying it closely when I heard—"I don't remember inviting you, Josiah."

Without missing a beat, I replied, "I came as Lady Elsmere's plus one since it was obvious my invitation got lost in the mail." I turned to face Ferrina. "That's a pretty heavy necklace you're wearing there, Ferrina. Sure it's not straining your neck muscles?"

"Is that your not-so-clever way of saying my necklace is gaudy?"

"No, ma'am. I never say a necklace with that many carats is gaudy. It's impressive and stunning." And it was in a frightening sense like the act of an avenging angel would be terrible to witness—beautiful and horrible at the same time.

Ferrina's face relaxed as she fingered the diamond and emerald stones surrounding her neck. "Why should June have the only diamond and emerald necklace on the social circuit? Besides, none of my stones are blood diamonds."

"It's true that the Elsmere's diamond and emerald necklace has a sordid past, but she inherited the diamond mine from her late husband, Lord Elsmere. Thanks to June, all the workers are now paid above the wage scale for South Africa and get a percentage of anything they find of gem quality. Since she took over the mine, there has not been one strike or protest concerning her policies."

Ferrina pursed her lips.

I needed to put out the fire I was stoking. "You *are* like Lady Elsmere in many ways, Ferrina."

Ferrina's eyes brightened. "Really? In what way?"

"You both are born leaders. Here you are, seeing a need for our working Thoroughbreds and finding a solution. Owners should be held accountable for what they do with their retired horses after their careers are over and not just racing horses, but draft horses and show horses, too."

Ferrina cocked her head to one side, assessing whether or not I was mocking her. Deciding to take my words at face value, she smiled. It must have been hard for her to smile with all the Botox injected into her face, but she gave it a mighty try. I wanted to close my eyes, afraid her pumped-up red lips might split open as her smile widened, so I trained my eyes on hers. I had to admit Ferrina did ferocious cat-eye makeup that went well with her leopard print halter dress and her tawny hair. Of course, she never complimented me about the way I looked, but she did offer some useful advice. "Ellen is here. I would consider it a personal favor if you would stay away from her. I'm trying to accomplish something important tonight. I don't need the two of you hissing at each other like two alley cats in front of the Bluegrass hoi polloi."

I drew back as I was impressed that Ferrina even knew the phrase hoi polloi. "I assure you that it won't be me who starts up anything."

Ferrina narrowed her cat eyes.

It wasn't exactly a promise but it was the best I could do.

"Good. Please excuse me. My other guests need my attention." Off Ferrina went, swishing away.

I could swear she must have had work done on her tush as well as her face. It was a formidable behind. I must admit I was a tad jealous because I certainly needed some freshening up. Who doesn't after the age of fifty?

Sighing, I turned back to study the Carolyn Hisel painting when I heard a familiar voice.

"Who do you think you are? Holly Golightly?"

It was Ellen. My head drooped. Here was the confrontation I had been dreading.

Oh, my nose just got longer. You know I'm lying. I love confrontations with Ellen and had secretly hoped our paths would cross tonight, but I swore to my daughter to be civil if I ran into Ellen. I don't consider what I said to Ferrina a promise, although it wasn't me who had crossed the room with a nasty intention. I had to admit, though, I was impressed that Ellen recognized I was copying Audrey Hepburn's iconic look in *Breakfast at Tiffany's*. I slowly turned. "Ellen, I just promised Ferrina not to start up anything with you tonight. Let's call a truce, okay?"

"You were not sent an invitation on purpose, so why are you here?"

"I'm Lady Elsmere's plus one."

"You're like a bad penny. Always turning up."

Ellen was the second person who had said that to me. Hadn't Detective Drake referred to me as a bad penny, too? I held up my hands in supplication. "Look. I don't want to cause any trouble. Lady Elsmere will tire soon, and we'll go home. I'll be out of your hair, but if you start any trouble with me, Ellen, she won't give a dime to this charity. Won't that make your best friend Ferrina angry, especially since she has gone to all this trouble? I mean this soiree cost a pretty penny, right?"

Ellen hesitated. What I said must have struck a chord with her. She shot me a contemptuous look but before she could pull away, I grabbed her arm. "Ellen, actually I'm glad we bumped into each other."

"Why?"

"Asa wants to see Brannon Jr."

"Never," Ellen hissed.

"Let's put our differences aside. You and I hate each other. I get that, but Brannon Jr. and Asa are brother and sister."

"Half-brother and sister."

"Let's not quibble. Brannon Jr. is the only sibling Asa will ever have. You can supervise the visit. She has never seen him."

Ellen laughed bitterly. "No doubt she did when she stole the Duveneck painting from my house."

"My husband should never have given that painting to you. I bought it as a gift. Brannon should have left it behind."

Ellen smiled. "Are you admitting Asa stole the painting?"

"No, Ellen. I have no idea where the painting is. Are you saying that if the painting miraculously turns up, then you'll let Asa see her brother?"

"I'm saying that without the return of the painting Asa will never see her brother."

"Ellen, must you be so vindictive?"

"The painting, Josiah, or I won't even consider letting Asa see my son." Ellen's eyes narrowed and her smile was a trembling orange slash across her face. The color did not suit her.

I knew Ellen loathed me, and it was more than the general dislike two women have for each other when competing for a man. She never forgave me for not letting her see Brannon in the hospital when he had his heart attack. Ellen would never see my side in this matter. She would never understand how devastated I was to learn of Brannon's affair, secretly selling our business, and then hiding the money from the sale when he decided to leave me. On top of that, Brannon had drained all our bank accounts.

After Brannon's death, I could never find out where he had stashed our money that I had worked years to save. I had a very strong suspicion he gave Ellen all the money from our bank accounts and business sale to hide during the divorce proceedings.

It was one thing to leave me. It was another thing for Brannon to leave me destitute and penniless while he lived the high life with his girlfriend. I was still his wife, and I needed Ellen to stay out of the picture until I got things settled with Brannon. Unfortunately, he up and died on me before there was any resolution between us. So there was no forgiveness—just a deep, abiding anger that is always rekindled when I see Ellen.

She gave me one last disdainful glance before hobnobbing with other guests. To tell you the truth, the woman unnerved me. I don't know why I always engage with her. Perhaps I'm a bit of a masochist.

Feeling discombobulated, I needed a few minutes to myself so I let myself into a room off the main corridor. I sat in a chair by the fireplace breathing slowly. When I finally regained my composure, I looked about and realized I must be in King's personal office. Now I was faced with a quandary. Do I join the other guests or do I use this opportunity to snoop?

I chose snooping.

There was a distinguished oil painting of King in his early fifties hanging over the ornate stone fireplace. King had been quite handsome before his recent illness. I gauged the portrait had been done right around the time he had married Ferrina. The room hosted expensive pale colored paneling with massive windows on one side that looked over the pool area and an expansive garden. On either side of the fireplace were shelves housing awards, personal mementos, and trophies of King's travels and triumphs. Each shelf was beautifully lit to highlight each object. The other walls showcased his first edition books and also a small bar offering only the finest ports and liquors. Off to the right was a private bathroom with a shower. Two club chairs sat in front of the fireplace with a 1930's Art Deco ashtray stand resting in-between. This was King's sanctuary where he came to smoke his cigars and have a glass of port, perhaps to reminisce about his past and get away from Ferrina.

The only other furniture in the room was a desk that hardly looked used. I tried the drawers. They were locked. The only item on the desk besides a lamp was a photograph of Ferrina. The photo must have been taken when they got married. She looked so young but not fresh, and Ferrina was smiling but not with her eyes. Something about the photograph bothered me. That's when it hit me.

The smiling Ferrina in the picture was the same wan face on the arrest warrant that Shelby Carpenter had in his possession. Wealthy, socially prominent Ferrina Landau was once the teenage prostitute and drug mule Susan Dorsch!

Jumping Jehoshaphat!

The door suddenly opened causing me to swirl. "Hello, King," I said.

Looking displeased, King asked, "May I help you, Josiah?"

"To tell you the truth, King, I came in here to get away from Ellen Boudreaux."

King relaxed and chuckled. "Ellen is a might over-powering. I would have done the same thing myself."

"While I was hiding in here, I spied this picture of Ferrina. It's lovely."

King strode over to where I stood. He picked up the sterling frame and studied the photograph of his wife. "This was Ferrina's engagement picture. It's my favorite of her."

"How old was she?"

"Twenty-four."

"How did the two of you meet?"

"You're going to think this is a cliché, but I met her on a trip to Las Vegas. My first wife had died in a car accident."

"I didn't know that. Very sorry for your loss."

"Thank you but we weren't very close. We never had children and through the years we drifted apart. I suppose if she hadn't died in the accident, we would have divorced. I'm sure of that. Neither one of us was happy. She was a nice woman, but we didn't click. Understand?"

I nodded, but I didn't understand. Hadn't June told me that King had married a friend of hers and she divorced him? Had King married three women? Was he rewriting his biography? Was he confused? Who was he yammering about? I decided to play along.

"I had to go to Las Vegas for a business conference, and I was dreading it. I got there a day early with nothing to do, so I went to a casino to play blackjack."

"You really wanted to lose some money," I joked.

King smiled. "I was playing when this angel slid into the chair next to me. We played a few hands. I won once and she won three times. Really got my attention."

"I bet," I murmured.

"She made a little pile of money and was gathering her chips when I asked if I could take her to dinner. She said yes and the rest is history. I know people think she married me for my money since she is almost thirty years younger, but Ferrina didn't know who I was when she accepted my invitation. I married Ferrina one month later and haven't had a day when I regretted it."

It was amazing to me that King had never figured out that he was a mark. Men are so gullible if there is a pretty face behind the lie. "That's quite a story, King."

"Ferrina gave me a son and saved me from a life of loneliness."

"Is Chase here today?"

"He's around somewhere. Probably twisting the arm of some pretty girl."

I thought that an odd metaphor to use but didn't reply. I also thought it was odd that there were no pictures of Chase in the room. I patted his arm in sympathy. "I'm glad it worked out for you, King. Please excuse me. I feel I have intruded upon your privacy long enough."

"Think nothing of it. I have nothing but time anymore, Josiah. Nothing but time."

I thought that also an odd thing to say since King was running out of time. Even the rich can't buy more days.

"You'd better go and lasso that beau of yours. He's chatting up all the ladies."

"Excuse me?"

"Hunter. He's working the room. Better corral Hunter while you can. You don't want him to run off, too."

Talk about pouring salt into a wound. Thanks, you old coot. I lost any feeling of sympathy for King. "I'm glad Hunter's enjoying himself. Please excuse me."

"Of course," King said with a little bow.

I left the room with more information than I had bargained for. I knew Susan Dorsch and Ferrina were one and the same person. Shelby Carpenter's death was directly related to Ferrina. Did Ferrina kill Carpenter to keep him quiet about her infamous past? I couldn't believe it. While such a revelation would have caused some twittering among Ferrina's friends, would anyone really care? Ferrina's colorful past would make her more of a star in this promiscuous day and age.

And if King hadn't been aware of her sordid history, would its revelation be such a shock that he would leave Ferrina? After all, King was very ill and said he loved Ferrina. At this stage in King's life, would he rock the boat?

There was one more thing. After the killer had

thrown Carpenter into VeVe's car, the open trunk lid would have shielded him from view, so the killer would have had ample time to search the body. The murderer didn't bother to take the arrest record or the newspaper articles on King. Was something even more incriminating taken?

I still had the strong feeling that whatever happened to Carpenter had to do with those pieces of paper, but what? I stood in the hallway before stepping out onto the lawn where most of the guests had gathered. It was then I noticed Ferrina's son, Chase, lurking in the shadows, just like in mystery novels. "Chase, is that you?"

"Hello, Josiah."

I tried not to show my irritation. I so dislike shopkeepers and those under the age of forty calling me by my first name. I was taught it was rude to call people by their first names unless permission was granted. This familiarity is not tolerated in other countries where proper respect is demanded, but I was not here to dispute modern American customs. "Did you want to see your father? He's free now."

"What were you discussing with him?" Chase asked in a honeycombed voice.

I was taken aback by such a question. "Why should that concern you?"

"My father is ill and his mind is starting to wander. We don't want people taking advantage of him."

Was this little twerp accusing me of malfeasance? The best defense is offense. "I hear college is not working out for you." I had never liked Chase. I thought his lackadaisical demeanor spoke of laziness and turpitude.

Chase smirked. "I'm doing just fine, Josiah. How's renting the Butterfly to the petty bourgeoisie working out for you?"

"Fine. Fine. The petty bourgeoisie in this town pay their bills, and I laugh all the way to the bank."

The smirk on Chase's face faded into a mask of loathing. I seemed to have hit a nerve. It was well known in Lexington that Chase had debts all over town, and he frequented the gambling boats on the Ohio River. Ferrina was always racing after him with her checkbook.

"The party is that way," Chase said, thumbing behind him. "This part of the house is off limits to guests." He smiled.

Yuck. It was a sleazy smile meant to convey sincerity and friendliness but like his mother's smile, it never reached his eyes.

I tried to get by, but his bulk blocked the hallway. There was no way I was going to touch him while passing, so we stood facing each other in a kind of a standoff.

The door to the study opened and King walked out. Seeing Chase and me facing off, King barked, "Chase, come here."

Chase reluctantly obeyed and went to his father who pushed him into the study.

King said, "Please excuse us, Josiah. I need to talk with my son. I'll see you later at the party."

"Of course," I said. I walked away and glanced back, seeing that King was watching me. I turned the corner into the great foyer where people were still arriving.

Thinking King had time to go into his study and shut the door, I tiptoed down the hall, thinking I would be able to eavesdrop, but the study door was slung open. Peeping around the door, I discovered no one was about. King and Chase must have gone out through the study's French doors out into the garden.

Ah, poo. I hate being denied a chance to eavesdrop. Taking a deep breath, I followed the stream of guests making their way to the garden where the party was taking place. I stepped out onto the verandah, but not before swiping a flute of pink champagne off a tray and taking a swig. I had three unpleasant encounters, which made me realize that I wasn't liked in the Landau household. It was enough to shake a girl's confidence.

Over to the left I saw June holding court with her cronies. She waved to me wanting me to come over. I waved back but moved in the opposite direction. I wanted to see if Hunter was really attending or if King was making that up. My mind raced through several scenarios if it were true. Why would Hunter receive an invitation and not ask me to accompany him? Was he with someone else? If I did see him, should I say hello or discreetly disappear into the crowd?

I got waylaid several times by friends and had to play catch-up. I acted calmly, but my heart was racing, and I escaped from each person as soon as was humanly possible. After all, I didn't want to appear rude. Finally, I made my way to the back part of the garden where I spied Hunter sitting with several ladies, including Ellen Boudreaux. I felt like someone had taken a shovel and hit me in the head with it. It was similar to how I felt when confronting Brannon at the Keeneland Race Course about his affair and the missing money. Not only did Brannon say that he wanted a divorce but that he hated me. I have never gotten over my husband saying that to me. I'll be damned before I let another man make a monkey out of me.

Hunter casually looked up and seeing me, quickly turned away. Well, I guess that says it all.

Ellen saw me too and scooted closer to Hunter. Under my breath I called Ellen a very vulgar name which I will not repeat, but it's a word ladies don't utter out loud. There was no way I was going to let people know how deeply wounded I was, so I smiled and waved to Hunter before turning and chatting with little knots of people here and there. I should have been an actress. My conversation sparkled. My wit was unmatched. I stunned friends with my acumen. I was the hit of the party and exhausted by the effort to maintain the façade. I finally stumbled upon June—thank my lucky stars.

"You ready to go home?" I whispered.

Out of the corner of her mouth, she mumbled, "You've seen Hunter?"

"Yep?"

"Why didn't he bring you?"

"That's the sixty-four thousand dollar question."

"Oh, I see. In that case, I'm ready. Can you fetch Charles? He went inside for another helping at the buffet table."

"If Charles doesn't wish to leave, I can catch a cab."

"Don't be absurd. He's only eating so he doesn't have to interact with these fools. He can't stand them." June grabbed her cane. "Here, help me up. These legs of mine are as brittle as dry twigs."

As I was pulling June up, Ferrina popped by with a Cheshire grin on her face. "Leaving so soon?"

June said, "I'm afraid my old bones are tiring out, Ferrina. Thank you for the invite. I would say your party was a success."

Ferrina simpered while fingering her necklace.

"One more thing, Ferrina," June said.

"Yes, Lady Elsmere?"

"I expect Charles Dupuy to be placed on the board for your charity."

"The board positions have already been filled, Lady Elsmere."

"Make another seat available—that is if you want to see a check from me and have my farm participate in the housing of retired horses."

Ferrina's hand dropped from her necklace. "I'll see what I can do."

"Thank you. You know Charles loves animals. As he is the heir to my estate, Charles needs to be involved with all aspects of my holdings, including charity work. Good night to you." Lady Elsmere began making her way inside the house.

I was picking up June's purse when I heard Ferrina mutter, "Charles is nothing more than a chauffeur, and she wants me to put him on my board?"

I shot back without thinking, "What's that Dorothy Parker saying? You can bring a whore to culture, but you can't make her think? It's a play on the saying— you can lead a horse to water, but you can't make it drink."

Ferrina's eyes flashed angrily at me. "Who is Dorothy Parker and what's she to do with me?"

I smiled sweetly at Ferrina. "You're too precious, and honey, I hate to tell you this, but some of the stones in your necklace are paste. Looks like someone's been filching your gems and replacing them with fakes."

I left the house feeling somewhat rejuvenated.

Aren't I a stinker!

14

Several days later there was a banging on my front door.

Ooops! I had forgotten to change the entry code on my front gate.

"Josiah, open this door!" Hunter demanded.

Baby went to the door and scratched it before looking back at me.

"Come away, Baby. Hunter is no longer welcomed."

Anxious at the continued banging, Baby whimpered, pacing back and forth.

"Go away," I yelled. "You're upsetting Baby."

"You won't answer my calls or emails."

"Go talk to your new girlfriend Ellen Boudreaux."

"I don't know what you've gotten into your head about Ellen Boudreaux. Just give me a chance to explain about the party. You owe me that much."

"I owe you nothing," I yelled through the door. "Go away."

Watching the surveillance monitor, I saw Hunter

kick my front door and leave.

Quitter.

It wasn't ten minutes later when I got a call from Matt. "Jo, Hunter is at my house. He says he won't leave unless you speak with him. I really need you to get him out of my house. Emmeline is picking up on his negative vibes and getting fussy."

"His negative vibes? You really have gone California on me."

"Jo! Don't put me in the middle of this. I'm going to send Hunter back up to you. I think you should really talk with him. He's very distraught."

"I must have sunk to the lowest level of Dante's Inferno if I'm taking relationship advice from you."

"Ha ha," Matt said. I could hear Emmeline squealing in the background. Hunter must have been playing with her.

"Okay. Okay. Send Hunter back to the Butterfly. I'll talk with him but only because you asked me to."

I could sense the relief in Matt's voice when he said, "Good. He'll be there in a few minutes."

I hung up my landline phone and rushed to my bedroom to change my clothes and brush my hair. No woman wants to look like a charwoman when lording over a man who has come with hat-in-hand to grovel.

Ding dong.

I smiled triumphantly as I reached for the doorknob and quickly put on my most contemptuous face as I opened the door.

<h1 style="text-align:center">15</h1>

"**I** don't know why I need to bring you offerings, but obviously I've done something heinous, so here you go." Hunter thrust a large bouquet of red roses and an opened gift box of chocolate bourbon balls at me.

I looked askance at the open box of candy. "You ate your apology?"

"I needed the sugar." Hunter brushed by me, headed straight for my liquor cabinet, and poured himself three fingers of my best whiskey. "You want to tell me why I've been denied an audience with the queen of the realm?"

I threw the gifts on the breakfast island. "Oh, stop the BS. You know why."

"Because I didn't run over and kiss your feet at Ferrina's party? Did it ever occur to you that I was working? Ellen Boudreaux was feeding me a delicious piece of gossip when you did your voodoo death stare at us."

I jabbed a finger at his face. "First of all, you don't

do detective work. That's the police's venue. You make a report based on the information that is given to you by the police department."

Hunter folded his arms while rolling his eyes.

"Second—you were talking to Ellen, who's my worst enemy in the world. I told you to steer clear of her, and third—you never asked me to be your plus one to go to Ferrina's shindig. Everyone thinks we've broken up. If we have, you sure didn't inform me." I imitated Hunter by folding my arms and rolling my eyes. "Wait a minute. Wait a minute. Ah, yeah, that's already happened to me once before with my jerk of a husband."

"Yes, Ellen was trying to play me. She always does when we bump into each other."

"Boy, you are really giving me ammunition to dump your fanny."

"If you remember, we first met at Sandy Sloan's house because I was investigating the site of the fire. Hmm, Miss Britches? Nothing to say? I do investigate on my own."

"That was different," I said stubbornly.

Hunter unfolded his arms and reached out to me.

I slapped his hand away.

"I didn't take you because when I'm with you all my attention is on you, and I wouldn't be able to do my job properly."

I melted a little. Darn it!

"I was there to hear rumors, gossip, and small nuggets of information. It was quite possible someone there could have known something."

"You should have explained why you were not taking me. I would have understood."

"I didn't think I needed to. I knew for a fact that you weren't invited and would not be welcomed."

"How?"

"Ellen called me up and asked me to escort her to the party."

"And you accepted!"

"Of course not. I told her I might be out of town on that date and to ask someone else."

I was livid. "See. See. This is what I'm talking about. The little snake. Why can't she get a man of her own? She's always after mine."

"The other reason I didn't say anything is that I assumed we were not exclusive. You've never intimated that you wanted this relationship to go any further than what it is."

"Don't blame this misunderstanding on me, buddy."

Hunter continued, ignoring my last statement, "But since you said and I quote 'She's always after mine' meaning a man and thus me—does that mean you wish to upgrade our status?"

"What are you saying?" I hoped the man didn't mean marriage.

"Are you dating anyone else?"

"None of your beeswax," I replied.

"So you don't want us to be a couple? Then may I ask why you are so upset? If we are both free agents, I can attend any event with or without you. By the way, you never said anything to me about going to Ferrina's party yourself. You did exactly the same thing I did."

"I didn't receive an invitation," I said smugly. "I was Lady Elsmere's plus one."

"But you never mentioned it."

"I didn't think you were invited either and didn't want to hurt your feelings since I was going with June."

Hunter laughed. "You are such a liar, Josiah. You didn't want me to know that you were going to Ferrina's house to pry."

"Why would I want to?"

"Because you went through Shelby Carpenter's pockets and saw the newspaper clippings on King."

"I did no such thing," I protested.

"My goodness, you're a piece of work."

I challenged Hunter. "Let's say it's so, how did you come to that conclusion when I said otherwise?"

"I interviewed Veritas Noble. She said she left you alone with the body while she went to the police station for help."

"Only a block away."

"It would still give you enough time to search the body. I wonder what the police would find if they got a warrant for your phone? I know you. You have more curiosity than nine cats."

"Now you're accusing me of perjury. You're not endearing yourself to me, Hunter. What is it you really want?"

"What do I really want?" Hunter repeated.

"Is there an echo in here?"

Hunter pulled me over to the couch and pushing me down, sat beside me holding my hand. "I want this fight to end. I want you to stop being jealous of Ellen or any other woman."

"You don't have a great track record with women, Hunter. How many times were you married?"

"None of my marriages failed due to infidelity. Ask my ex-wives."

"What else?"

"I want us to be exclusive."

I didn't respond.

"If you are fond of me enough to be jealous, I think we should take our relationship up a notch."

"You're an unusual man asking for a commitment. Most men run for the door when the subject is brought up."

Hunter grinned. "I'm too old to play the dating game, Jo. Maybe I haven't told you, but I'm rather fond of you."

"Like you're fond of a well worn pair of house slippers?"

"You *are* rather well-worn, my dear."

"You're no catch yourself. You're broke. You don't have a steady job and what money you make is plowed into your *Tobacco Road* plantation."

"Wickliffe Manor, my ancestral home," Hunter said, correcting me. "I am going to save it, just like you saved the Butterfly. So, my dear, we are two people who understand each other. We connect."

"I hear a 'but' in there somewhere."

"Not a 'but.' It's an 'and.' I want to know what you think about this case with Shelby Carpenter."

"So that's what this is really about. You want to pick my brains."

Hunter said, "I've thought of a way for you to tell me what you know without placing yourself in any legal jeopardy."

Baby interrupted us by dropping a chewed-up squeaky toy in Hunter's lap, which he wanted Hunter to throw.

Hunter tossed it across the room.

Baby retrieved it and brought the soggy toy back only to drop it again in Hunter's lap. Looking expectantly at Hunter, Baby wagged his tail, thumping it against the couch.

Scratching Baby behind the ears, Hunter said, "Not now, Baby. Go lie down now. I'll play with you later."

Baby sneezed, reclaimed his toy, and lumbered over to his bed. Turning three times, he lay down, happily chewing on his toy.

How could I not care for a man who treated my dog with such respect the way Hunter did? Most people would have pushed Baby away or yelled at him. I asked, "What's your idea about the Carpenter case?"

Hunter's eyes lit up. "I'm going to hire you as my consultant. That way you can legally access the file on Carpenter."

"It would be a conflict of interest. I'm a witness."

"There's no law against this in the state of Kentucky."

"It doesn't look good. It would mar your reputation."

"I don't plan on anyone knowing of our arrangement, but I'm going to have a signed contract with you in case the matter comes up in court."

"I don't know, Hunter. It sounds rather dicey and underhanded."

"Since when did you become so particular?"

I smiled sweetly. "You are stumped on this case, and you want to know what I think."

"I want both you and your brain."

"Which puts me in the driver's seat."

"Name your terms, Machiavelli."

"Let's table the discussion about us for now. We both have a lot on our plates at the moment, and our relationship is something we should discuss when we are in a better frame of mind."

"I'll wait until I turn my report in. No longer."

"Agreed."

"And the other matter?"

"I'll sign your contract if you stipulate that you'll pay for any and all legal fees if I get in Dutch with the DA over working with you on this case."

"Sounds fair."

"Good. Good. Now how much are you going to pay me for my little gray cells?" I said, mimicking Hercule Poirot's Belgium accent.

"One dollar."

"Tightwad."

"You're already on shaky ground, Jo. Everyone working on this case thinks you searched the body. Drake has even suggested that you might have taken evidence. I am giving you a legal way out."

I didn't reply because I certainly wasn't going to incriminate myself.

Hunter scratched his forehead. "This didn't turn out to be the amorous makeup visit I envisioned."

"What did you think was going to happen?"

"I thought we would have a little verbal tussle, but in the end you would relent and fall into my arms."

"And then what?"

"I would kiss you madly and carry you into the bedroom for some heart pounding sex."

"Oh, you smooth talking devil."

We both laughed but I could tell Hunter was disappointed. I don't know why I wasn't taking him up on his heart pounding sex offer. I guess it was because I hadn't told him about my bum kidneys, and I wasn't ready to tell anyone yet. I was still praying for a miracle or perhaps I was in denial, but it wasn't right for Hunter to invest in this relationship without knowing all the facts. Still, I wouldn't give him up. I knew I should send Hunter on his way, but he was going to have to make that decision once I told him the truth about my health. I didn't have the moral fiber to do it myself.

Not yet, at least.

16

Several days later, Hunter laid his files on my Nakashima table and pulled out photographs of the crime scene. They were hard to gaze at even though there wasn't much blood. Still though, to see a man crumpled up in the trunk of someone's car—was not nice to look at. I winced.

"How can you possibly be squeamish looking at these pics when you saw the real thing?"

"I didn't like seeing that either. It was terrible to open the trunk and see this poor soul stashed like a sack of potatoes, and it's quite a jolt to see these photographs spread out on my dining room table as well."

"Should motivate you to help me."

"It does."

Hunter took a deep breath. "Let's get started. Everything you tell me will be confidential."

"Unless under oath."

"That is correct, Jo, but I will keep your involvement under wraps like I do with all my confidential informants."

"You have snitches?"

"Focus, Josiah. Focus."

"Has Carpenter's rental car been discovered?"

"Yes, it was found parked in the long term parking lot at the airport."

"That would make sense. The killer driver could drop off the car, get a cab at the airport, or walk across the road to Keeneland Race Course. What do the surveillance tapes show?"

Hunter pointed to a blurry picture. "A white male wearing dark glasses and a baseball cap. No identifying clothing or tattoos."

"Seems young though."

"How can you tell?"

"I don't know. Just a sense of how he carries himself."

"I think he's young, too. Like you, I sense it."

"What do the taxi drivers say?"

"It was a busy day. People were flying in for the races at Keeneland. Lots of young men with baseball caps."

"But I think this fare would take the perp back into town to retrieve his own car. Any fares downtown?"

"Gobs of them. All the hotels downtown were booked."

"Apparently no one aroused suspicion."

"And lots of people still pay by cash when riding in taxis."

I asked, "Did the police photograph the license plates of all the cars in a block radius of the crime scene?"

"They didn't feel the need to do so at the time. They thought it was a botched robbery attempt."

"Even with his wallet intact? Sloppy police work."

Hunter gave me a little satisfied smirk. "So you did search the body?"

"I was surmising. Was his wallet intact with cash and credit cards?"

"Clever, Josiah. You want me to tell you the facts of the case so you can say you made suppositions based on the information I gave you. Okay, I'll play. Yes, his wallet and money were found on his body."

"I bet the murderer's car was parked close by. It had to be if my theory is correct that Carpenter was being followed. All the police had to do was check the other cars."

I thought for a moment. "Was it confirmed that it was Carpenter's rental car that hit VeVe's car?"

"Yes. The police think the perpetrator rammed Carpenter's car which caused it to damage Noble's car."

I shook my head vehemently. "No. No. No. The perp's car did not cause this. I think Carpenter ran into VeVe's car by accident. Perhaps Carpenter realized he was being followed and became distracted thus causing the accident. The damage to Carpenter's car was only on the front, right?"

Hunter quickly perused a report. "Yes, the front on the driver's side."

"So for whatever reason, Carpenter became distracted and hit VeVe's car accidentally, but he feels safe enough to get out and check the damage. Being an honorable man, he leaves money for the repairs but doesn't leave any contact information because he's undercover for a story and doesn't want his presence in town known."

"Here's the problem with your hypothesis. If Carpenter thought someone was following him, why not drive on?"

"Maybe he wasn't positive. Maybe the accident rattled him. Have you read his work?"

"Yep."

"Then you see that Carpenter was a principled man."

"Again, that is supposition." Hunter asked, "What do you think happened?"

"Did it ever occur to you that Carpenter hit Veritas Noble's car on purpose? Perhaps he did realize he was being followed and felt threatened. He wanted to scare the perp away. What better way to do so than to create a commotion which would cause lots of people to gawk and even get the cops to show up?"

"So he randomly picks a car on a street where there is not much foot traffic? Sorry, but that seems farfetched to me. My distraction theory fits the facts better."

Hunter made notations on a yellow legal pad.

"Was anything missing from Carpenter's pockets?"

Flicking some lint off his jacket, Hunter made a face. "As if you didn't know. The police couldn't find his phone, and that's why they thought this murder to be a robbery gone bad at first."

"It was a robbery but not for money if Carpenter's wallet was left with cash and credit cards intact."

"He did have credit cards but we can find no record of him using them in the Bluegrass."

I said, "Credit cards give away the user's location. I bet Carpenter used cash when working on a story. No one can track him that way. It explains why he had the money to leave on VeVe's car."

"I guess."

"Everything points to Carpenter's death having to do with a story he was working on. He would have stored information on his phone. Reporters don't use pad and pencil anymore."

"Then why leave the police report and newspaper clippings?"

"Why do you keep asking me questions for which you've already developed a hypothesis?" I asked.

"I want to see if you think the same way I do on

this case. Come on. Give it up."

"Have the police found a laptop?"

"Yes, but it was wiped clean."

"I think everything that happened to Carpenter has to do with a story he was working on."

"Sure 'nough, but still doesn't explain why the police report and the newspaper clippings were left behind."

"Because paper is old school. A young perpetrator wouldn't have thought to look for such things. These young kids don't read newspapers. Don't use phone books or paper maps. They don't write checks. Don't write letters. Half of them don't even know how to address an envelope. They do everything electronically."

"I agree, which again points to a young assailant. Let's move on."

"May I see the police report Carpenter had in his pocket?"

Hunter handed me a copy of the report. He studied me closely as I pretended to study the report.

"Have the police done a background check on the girl mentioned in the report?" I asked.

"Came up with a dead end."

"They should look closer to home."

"What do you mean, Jo?"

I pointed to the mug shot. "This girl is Ferrina Landau."

"Noooo!" Hunter said, grabbing the report out of my hand. He peered closely at the picture. Looking up at me, he said, "I see it now. How could we have missed this?"

"Here's another odd thing. I ran into King at the party, and he related to me about how he met Ferrina playing blackjack in Las Vegas. He also made a reference to his former wife who died in a car accident. Now that story contradicts what June told me. She stated King married a friend of hers who divorced him."

"Maybe June is mistaken."

"Her mind is sharp as a tack while King has Parkinson's disease. However, I ran into his son, Chase, in the hallway. He was very unpleasant and inferred the family had to keep an eye on King because his mind wandered."

"You know Chase was kicked out of Centre College. Flunked out."

"This tells me that you have already connected the Landau family to the Carpenter case."

"What do you know about Chase Carpenter?" Hunter asked.

"He's a spoiled rich kid whose mommy and daddy always come to his rescue."

"I understand he likes to gamble."

"Yep."

"Would you say he lacks impulse control?"

"Right on," I replied.

"What about his intelligence?"

"Average I'd say."

"Has he ever shown any violence—acted out."

"I've never seen Chase become violent but he can't keep a girlfriend."

"Really?" Hunter said, making a notation. "Can you expand on that?"

"Not really. I'm not close to the family. Everything I know comes from June." I tried to decipher Hunter's handwriting upside down.

"Anything else you want to tell me?"

"No."

"Know any of Chase's girlfriends' names?"

"No, but I can find out."

"Do that, please. Today, if possible. I need to turn in my report tomorrow."

"So you are honing in on Chase?"

"I think there is a possible connection with the Landaus and Shelby Carpenter."

"Find Carpenter's phone. Then you'll have your answers."

"That phone could be at the bottom of the Kentucky River for all we know." Hunter grimaced and straightened his files. "Mind if I stay here and work. It will save me time."

"Go ahead. I'll give you some privacy. I have to check on my bees."

"Shall I lock up when I leave?"

"Please do. I'm taking Baby with me."

Hunter reached over and gave me a peck on the lips. "Dinner tonight?"

"I'll pass if you don't mind. I'm not feeling up to snuff."

"Anything wrong?" Hunter looked concerned.

"Nothing that getting a good night's rest won't cure. I'll call you this evening."

"Okay."

"Sounds like a plan." I rose from the table. "I'll talk to you later."

"All right."

I could feel Hunter watch me as I called for Baby and left the house. I'm sure he watched me get into my golf cart on the monitors.

I didn't lie. I did check on the bees where I found one of my peacocks was perched atop a hive. "That's a dangerous place to roost," I cautioned, but the peacock paid me no mind.

He let out a loud cry, which sounded like a woman screaming. I loved the sound of it. For some reason, peacock cries calm me. I liked to hear their piercing screams, but judging from the complaints I get from neighbors, I was the only one who did.

I filled up water containers where I had placed pebbles and marbles for the bees. Unlike wasps and other insects, honey bees can't drink while flapping their wings. They must find a safe platform from which to drink or they will drown, so I have water stations about the farm and especially near the hives. I change their water frequently, especially during the summer when they need more water to cool down the hive.

The hives looked in great shape. Bees were making their way from the fields where I had not mowed. Abundant pollen and nectar from the goldenrod were now blooming. In a week or so, I would harvest the last batch of honey and get the hives ready for winter. Honey made from the goldenrod nectar would be darker and have a sharper taste than the spring honey.

Five guard honey bees emerged from a hive and tried to chase me off by buzzing around my face, threatening to sting me. Since I didn't want to be stung, I quickly retreated, resisting the urge to swat them away. If hit, the bees release a chemical that says to the other bees, "Help! I'm being attacked," causing their sisters to rush to their rescue.

I wrapped my hands around my face since the last thing I wanted was a bee to sting my eyes or accidentally wind up in my ears or nose. Scurrying off in my golf cart, Baby and I made a clean getaway.

Baby barked ferociously and snapped at the air.

"Yes, I know, Baby. They are in a foul mood today," I concurred, making a mental note to recheck that hive in a couple of days. If the guards from the same hive were still aggressive, I would have to suit up and open the hive. Sometimes bees were anxious because the queen was injured, the hive was sick, or starving. A quick fix with emergency sugar water might be all that was needed. Other times, medicine was required.

If the queen was dead or injured, I would combine the distressed hive with a healthy hive. It was a simple procedure that allowed both hives to thrive. I would open the top of a healthy hive and put newspaper on the top hive body with slits cut into the paper. Then I would place the hive bodies from the distressed hive on top of the newspaper allowing bees from both sides to chew their way through to each other. By the time they met, the bees from the distressed hive would accept their new queen, and the two groups of bees would merge together in harmony. Most of the time, this procedure worked well, providing a large, healthy hive to get through the Kentucky winter.

Another technique was to place the distressed hive on top of a closed healthy hive. The heat from the healthy hive would help the distressed hive survive until spring when I could place a new queen into the distressed hive and move it to a new location. I wouldn't know what to do until I went into the hive to see the reason for the bees' bad temper.

I had cut down on the number of hives on the farm. There were only thirty hives now from which I harvested sixty to a hundred pounds of honey per year, and I usually sold out every Saturday I attended the farmers' market. The money from charging ten dollars for a pound of honey paid my household bills. Thirty hives were a good number for me because I didn't need a lot of help with them which kept my costs down. I hired Charles' grandsons, Malcolm or Tyrone, to help with the lifting. I just couldn't lift those heavy hive boxes anymore. A bottom hive body with honey, pollen, and baby bee brood could weigh anywhere from sixty to eighty pounds. Too much for me.

Now that Matt was home, perhaps I could wrangle him into helping in exchange for some babysitting. Free labor would certainly help my bottom line. I decided to approach Matt about it as he would be home early today, but at the moment I needed to see Charles. I knew he was at one of the equine nursery barns. Some of the hay given to a mare had caused her to become sick, so Charles was checking the feed for the mares. I looked for a veterinarian's van alongside Charles' SUV and found them at barn #3.

I sidled up alongside Charles, who was watching the vet examine the mare. "How's she doing?"

"We got her up on her feet, but I'm not happy about this," Charles said, looking worried.

"Was it bad hay?" Sometimes mold grew in hay making an animal sick.

The vet looked up. "Hi Josiah."

"Hi Jordan."

"Well?" Charles asked.

Jordan pulled off his gloves. "I don't think it was the hay. I think she's eaten something like paper or plastic. I'll give her something to wash it out of her system. Keep a close watch on her and check her manure. If this doesn't help, we might have to operate."

Charles stomped his foot in anger. "I hate it when people litter. They throw their drink cups and fast food wrappers out on the road, and it blows into our pasture where the horses eat them. Makes me so mad."

"You've got to have your men patrol your fields," Jordan said, pouring disinfectant on his hands.

"They patrol twice a day now. I'll step it up to three times."

Jordan said, "I don't know why people litter on our beautiful roads either. Makes us look dirty to the tourists." He thought for a moment. "Might consider putting wire on the fences facing Tates Creek so the trash won't blow into the fields."

"Hate to do that since we are stepping up tours on the farm. People come expecting to see three plank horse fences."

Jordan shrugged while gathering his instruments. "Don't know what to tell you other than to put up surveillance cameras and try to catch whoever is throwing out the trash. Might be the same person. After paying a five-hundred dollar fine for littering, he might think twice about chucking out a soft drink bottle."

"Or he may shoot one of the horses out of revenge," Charles commented. "I don't know what's wrong with folks nowadays. No respect. None at all. Don't people realize that this farm employs forty people and pumps four million dollars into the local economy every year? No respect, I tell you. None."

Jordan gathered his bag. "Call me if there is any change in her condition."

"Will do."

As soon as Jordan got into his van, Charles turned to me and said, "I'm going to call Velvet Maddox and have her come over to do her voodoo thing."

"Don't call it voodoo around Velvet. It's old timey wise-woman mountain tradition handed down from mother to daughter according to her."

Charles grinned. "I don't care what it's called. That witchy woman always makes animals feel better. I should have called her first." He pulled out his phone and began to dial but stopped, glancing at me. "I don't know what's wrong with me. Where are my manners? Josiah, did you come over here for a reason?"

"Yeah. I was wondering if you could help me. You stated in the car driving over to Ferrina's that you had contacts through the employees of most of the big houses in the Bluegrass."

"That's right. Best news network there is."

"Could you ask around and find out any scuttlebutt about the Landaus and especially Chase? I'd like to know who he's dated and why they broke up."

"I'll ask around but don't mention this to Miss June. She wouldn't like it."

"I thought June encouraged gossip. That's how she knows everything going on in Lexington."

"Miss June only likes it if the information is for her ears alone. She wouldn't like me to gather intel for you. Understand the nuances here?"

I rolled my eyes. "Anything to keep Her Ladyship happy. I don't want her barking up my tree."

"Give me a couple of days."

"Okay. Just leave a message on my machine and mums the word." Charles and I bumped fists.

Afterwards, I hurried to find Baby. He had wandered back home where I found him in my horse barn sleeping on some oat feed sacks. Leaving Baby to sleep, I stopped by Morning Glory's stall. She stuck her head out for her ears to be scratched. I fed her some sweet hay and gave her a quick rub down. "How ya doing, girl?" I leaned against Glory's neck and inhaled the pony's musky scent, fondly remembering the day when Hunter gave her to me. I also remembered the day she jumped over a fence knocking me off the saddle backwards. Since then I have been afraid to ride Glory, but I won't give her up. She's my pal. Her muzzle felt soft on my palms as I fed her one last handful of oats before going back home, hoping to find Hunter gone.

He was.

I felt relieved, and that disturbed me.

17

I didn't hear from Hunter for several days. He called to say he was in Louisville working on another case and wouldn't be back until next week. When I asked about the Shelby Carpenter case, Hunter related that he had turned his profile report in, and that Ferrina, King, and Chase were questioned. No physical evidence connected them to the murder as they all had alibis at the time of Carpenter's attack. The Carpenter killing seemed likely to evolve into a cold case as most murderers are discovered and booked within forty-eight hours after the crime has been committed. I was disappointed to say the least. If the Landaus weren't involved, I had no leads myself. I just couldn't shake the feeling they were somehow mixed up in this mess.

"Was Ferrina identified as the girl in the police arrest report?" I asked.

"Seems so."

"Did King know his wife had a previous life as a call girl and drug mule?"

"Don't know. They were questioned after I turned in my report."

"Can you take the cops who worked on the case for a couple of beers and pry some information from their lips? It should be easy, you being a head jockey and all."

"Head jockey? Now that's a new term I've never heard before regarding my profession." Hunter chuckled. "I'll nose around a little when I get back."

"Is Franklin back from New York?"

"Yes, and I told him that Matt is back."

"How did he react?"

"Didn't say much. Went out on a date a couple hours later. Has he called you about Matt?" Hunter asked.

"Haven't heard a peep from him."

"I think Franklin needs time. Perhaps he's decided to move on. I hope so. I think Matt is bad for him."

"Since Franklin hasn't reached out to me, I won't call him."

"Yeah. He probably needs some space."

I heard a knock on the hotel door over the phone.

"That must be room service. I'll call you when I get back to Lexington."

"Okay. Make sure you look through the peephole before you open the door," I cautioned.

"Talk to you later."

"Bye," I said, but I was talking to a dead line. I put

the phone up and pondered what Hunter had written in his report regarding Shelby Carpenter. He may have come to some conclusion, but I hadn't. It was time to see if Charles had made contact with employees from the Landau house. I called to Baby, and we walked to the Big House.

June was taking a nap, so it was the perfect opportunity to talk with Charles over a piece of Bess' apple strudel and a glass of milk. "Do you have anything for me?"

Charles handed me a page of notebook paper with handwritten names. "This is a list of ladies Chase has squired about town. I have their addresses but no phone numbers."

"Wow. This is quite a roll. Is there a special lady—someone that he took a shine to?"

"That would be Diane Voss. He dated her the longest."

"What happened?"

"She dumped him."

"Why?" I wondered.

"You'll have to ask her. She works at the Tates Creek library evenings."

"Just evenings?"

"She's going to school full time."

"What else did your connections say?"

"Nothing unusual. Ferrina is difficult to please while Chase is amazingly clean and tidy."

"Didn't see that coming," I deadpanned. "What else?"

"King has a separate bedroom from Ferrina since his health has been declining."

"Are they solid?"

"My connection said Ferrina dotes on him but her real affection is for Chase."

"What about Chase and King?"

"Some friction there as to be expected when the heir does not meet the father's expectations. I understand King took it hard when Chase flunked out of college."

"Anything strange going on like drug or alcohol abuse?"

"I know you have heard stories about Chase's gambling problem."

I nodded. "Yes, I think everyone has heard rumors about it."

"The rumors are true. He owed thirty thousand until Ferrina bailed him out, but apparently there was a big row when King found out."

"How did he?"

"He still checks all the financial statements for the house, personal, and business accounts. It's tough to get anything past him. King's a sharp old bird."

"Chase said his mind was going."

Charles replied, "I think Chase would like to think so."

"When I talked to King, his mind was very clear except for one thing. King said his wife died in a car accident. June said her friend married King and then divorced him. Did King have more than one wife before Ferrina?"

"It would be easy enough to find out, Josiah. Just go on the Internet. Everything is on there."

"Thanks, Charles. I owe you one."

"I've gotta scoot. Velvet Maddox is coming to look at that mare."

"She bringing her dowsing rods?"

"I hope so. The horse is not responding to treatment. I've got to do something."

"Say hey to Velvet for me."

Bess looked up from snapping green beans. "You coming for dinner, Dad?"

"Honey, can you make me and your mother a plate to take back to our house? Your mother's not feeling well, and I don't want to tax her."

"I'll make a basket and bring it over. All you'll have to do is heat it up. That way I can check on Mother. Should I call a doctor?"

"Went to the clinic this morning. We won't know anything until the tests come back, but it's nothing to worry about, honey."

I didn't say anything but I saw alarm register on Bess' face. We both knew Charles was downplaying his wife's possible declining health.

Bess glanced at me.

I mouthed, "Let it go." There was no use giving Charles the third degree until the test results came in.

Bess must have agreed. She cleared away the kitchen table, and Charles went into his office.

I gave Bess a quick hug and left with Baby. I pushed negative thoughts aside and concentrated on questioning Diane Voss. It's better to be busy when faced with possible unpleasantness. That's always my plan.

Walking home, Baby and I checked on the hive whose guards chased me. Everything seemed normal, and there were no stains on the front of the hive. Brown stains on the front of a hive could signal dysentery—a serious problem but treatable. No guards chased us. I bent down and looked into the opening where I saw many guards peering back, but none pursued me.

We walked past Matt's little bungalow. It was locked up tight as Matt had found a job, and Emmeline was in daycare. On Tuesdays and Thursdays Matt worked long hours at the law firm, and I would gather Emmeline from daycare to stay with me until he got home. If Matt was very late, Emmeline slept at my house until he came for her the next morning, so now the Butterfly was littered with toys, bottles, and baskets of laundry I washed for Matt.

While babies are not my favorite thing, Emmeline and I had grown accustomed to each other, and she enjoyed spending time with me. My favorite activity was to read to Emmeline. I was going to make sure Emmeline had an expanded vocabulary.

Wait a minute. I did that with my daughter, Asa, and look how she turned out—mercurial and furtive! I'm sure she got those traits from her father.

"Come on, Baby. I have to get you back home because I need to get to the library to get more books."

Like I said—it's always better to be busy when faced with doubts.

I had a lot of doubts about Shelby Carpenter's death.

Perhaps a trip to the library would alleviate them and soothe my mind.

18

There were several young women working at the Tates Creek Library branch, but only one that looked like someone Chase would date—someone flashy. She was working alone at the reference desk.

I meandered over with my arm full of books. "Excuse me. Can you point me in the direction of any book on St. Hildegard of Bingen?"

The young woman blinked and said, "Oh, yes. Over at the historical section, third row from the bottom on the left side. We have several books on her. You should also check out our music CD's. She was an amazing composer as well. Sister Hildegard is one of my favorite women from the medieval period."

"She's one of mine, too." I looked quizzically at the librarian as if remembering her and asked, "Did you ever date Chase Landau? I'm a friend of his mother, Ferrina."

The girl seemed taken back.

"You're Diane Voss." I readjusted my books and

stuck out my hand. "I'm Josiah Reynolds."

Diane shook my hand. "I've heard of you. You're in the paper a lot. Didn't you find a dead body in a car recently?"

"The trunk to be exact."

"Yes. The reason I remember your name is that I thought you were a man. Josiah was a king in the Old Testament, wasn't he? I thought the paper was wrong referring to you as 'she' until someone told me that you are a woman."

"Guilty as charged."

"How is it you know who I am again?" Diane asked.

"I'm a friend of Ferrina's. In fact, I saw Chase earlier this month at a party his mother threw. As a friend of Chase's, I know you must be concerned that he is no longer welcomed at Centre College."

"Chase and I no longer date, so I'm not privy to any issues at college."

"That's a shame since Ferrina told me she thought you and Chase made such a cute couple."

Diane's face screwed up into a tiny ball. "Excuse me. I must get back to work. The books you want are over there," she said, thumbing behind her.

Uh oh. "Did I say something wrong, dear?"

Diane looked at me with intense dislike. "I don't know what game you're playing but I doubt very much Ferrina thought Chase and I made a 'cute couple.' The woman positively loathed me."

"Ferrina must have had a change of heart."

"Please go away," Diane pleaded, looking around. "I need this job."

"Then smile while we're talking." I put my books down on the reference desk. "I don't mean to make trouble. Really, I don't. I found Shelby Carpenter's body, and I'm trying to tie up loose ends."

"Are you a cop?"

"Not exactly, but I have a vested interest."

"How can I possibly help you? I don't know any Shelby Carpenter."

"I was wondering why you stopped dating Chase Landau."

"What business is that of yours? If you don't leave right now, I'm going to call security," Diane said, her voice filled with anger.

"Just answer the question, and I'll leave. Promise."

"He was a jerk. All right? Now go, please."

Boy, I was really suave at interrogating Diane, wasn't I?

Diane tried to get the attention of another librarian, so I knew it was time to leave. I gathered my books, checked out, and hurried to my Prius. I was afraid to look back to see if incensed librarians were running after me with pitchforks and torches. I must have hit a nerve, but then again, I was being pushy.

I seem to have a knack for it.

19

You're going to think I'm a terrible person. I knew Hunter was going to be away for several more days, so I went to Wickliffe Manor and let myself in with a spare key Hunter hid under a rock. I called out for Franklin even though I knew his little Smart Car was gone. I assumed he was at work.

Making my way to Hunter's study, I went through his filing cabinet, which I opened with my new set of picklocks that Asa gave me for my birthday. Isn't my daughter thoughtful? You might think Hunter was old school for still having a filing cabinet and paper files, but Hunter and I are old enough not to trust computers. We always have paper backup.

Bingo!

I found Shelby Carpenter's file. I grabbed it and sat at Hunter's desk perusing it. I studied Carpenter's autopsy report. He had been shot in the back of the head with a .22 caliber gun. It would seem Carpenter was facing away from his attacker when shot, so he may not have even known he was in danger. If one has to die by misadventure, that's the way to go. You don't even see it coming. According to the autopsy, there was no other damage to the body.

Looking through the different records in the file, I found the report on the cars. It *was* Carpenter who hit VeVe's car. The police lab matched the paint from Carpenter's rental to VeVe's car. I felt a little glimmer of satisfaction. I was right about who hit whom.

The rest of Hunter's report was subjective and open to interpretation of the evidence. He suggested my theory of what happened after the accident. Carpenter puts money under VeVe's windshield wiper and goes back to close the trunk which had popped open during the accident. As he is standing near the trunk, he is shot. He falls to the ground or slumps halfway into the trunk. The murderer pushes him all the way into the trunk, checks Carpenter's pockets, takes the dead man's phone, and closes the trunk. Then he simply gets into Carpenter's vehicle and drives away, leaving his own transportation close by which he retrieves later.

I knew how, but the why and who was missing. I greedily read Hunter's profile. Hunter thought the attacker was a young, athletic, white male with considerable upper body strength. The attack was simple and without anger or passion. Hunter posed the strong possibility that Carpenter's demise could have been a for-hire killing since the phone was missing and his laptop, found in the back seat of the rental, had been sabotaged. I can see why Hunter thought this murder to be an execution. Professional hit men favored head shots with as little fuss as possible.

I slumped back in Hunter's chair. The case might never be solved if a professional had killed Carpenter. The key to this case was the story Carpenter had been working on but what was it? I still believed it had something to do with the Landaus, especially Chase. Chase was my number one suspect even though I thought it weak that he could carry out such an efficient murder and not get caught. So why did I have Chase at the top of my list?

The question Hunter would ask is—if that were true why would Chase leave Ferrina's police report and newspaper clippings about King? My answer would be the same as before—young people don't think about paper. They are about electronics.

As for a professional hit, my answer would be that the murderer was acting through a mediator and was told only to take Carpenter's phone and destroy the laptop. The fact that Carpenter had folded-up paper reports in his pocket is not something that occurred to anyone. The assassin might not have even known the Landaus had ordered the hit.

There. Two possible explanations of who did the dirty deed.

Now—as to the why.

20

VeVe and I were having dinner at a little café near her house.

"You look tired, VeVe."

"I'm not sleeping well. Ever since we found Mr. Carpenter, I've been having nightmares. I even sleep with the light on. I jump at every sound. It's unnerving. Has this been happening with you?"

"Nah. I sleep like a baby."

"Oh."

"I don't mean to sound insensitive, but this is not my first rodeo."

"You have been stepping over dead bodies quite a bit lately. Why is that, Jo? You used to be so normal."

"I do seem to stumble over the dark side of people. I keep hoping it's a phase."

VeVe smiled. "I used to think it was so glamorous of you solving all these mysteries, but now that I have been involved in one, it feels . . ."

"Sordid?"

Blushing, VeVe nodded. "No offense intended."

"None taken. I know what you mean."

"Did the police make you take a lie detector test?"

I looked up curiously from my chicken salad. "No. Why?"

"They made me take one, and they have asked me to come in for another talk. I don't think they believe me when I said I didn't know this Shelby Carpenter."

"Do you have an appointment scheduled with the police?"

"Day after tomorrow."

I pulled Shaneika Mary Todd's business card from my wallet and handed it to VeVe. "Tell Shaneika that you are a friend of mine and ask her if she will go with you to the police interview. She is the number one criminal lawyer in the state."

"What do the police want from me? Why should I need a lawyer?"

"They want to rattle your cage and see what falls out. They have no other suspect, and you are the closest person at hand. They're just fishing."

VeVe poked at her salad in contemplation.

"What is it? Something else is troubling you?"

She put down her fork and used her paper napkin to dab her eyes. "Josiah, this murder might cause me to go bankrupt. The police impounded my car and the thousand dollars Carpenter left. The police won't release either, and I need my car for work." VeVe used her napkin to blow her nose.

"Don't cry, VeVe."

"I don't know what I'm going to do, Jo. I can't afford Miss Todd. I simply can't."

"She'll let you pay so much a month. The expense for the interview shouldn't be too much, and Shaneika will stop future harassment. She'll be worth the few hundred dollars you'll pay her."

VeVe took a deep breath. "You think I should take her?"

"I do, VeVe. I think you're getting in over your head. Shaneika will help you find solid ground." I knew how VeVe felt. I had been in her shoes once when a rogue cop hounded me for years and almost murdered me at Cumberland Falls. VeVe needed some backup and fast.

VeVe gingerly put the card in the front pocket of her purse.

"If the police have your car, how did you get here?"

"In a rental, but I can't keep that up. It's too costly but I've got to have transportation for work." VeVe mopped her eyes again. "Why does everything have to be so hard. Why won't the police release my car? I'm so angry I could spit."

"Because your car is evidence, and they haven't solved the case yet." I pulled a checkbook from my purse and wrote a check for a thousand dollars. "Pay me twenty dollars at the first of each month."

VeVe pushed my outstretched hand away. "I can't take that. It would make my insomnia worse knowing that I owed someone a thousand dollars. Besides, you need that money yourself."

I could see there was no use pressing the issue. "Very well. I'm sure they'll release your car as soon as they arrest someone." Of course, I didn't believe that for one second.

"I wish they'd get on with it. If I could do something to solve this case myself, I would. I hate feeling this helpless." VeVe stabbed a tomato repeatedly.

"I think your salad is dead, VeVe." I commented, before coming up with a brilliant idea. "Why don't you ask Lady Elsmere if you can borrow one of her farm trucks until the police release your car?"

"I can't do that. I don't know her very well."

"But I do. The farm has lots of trucks. I'm sure they could spare one."

VeVe shook her head. "I don't know how to drive a stick shift."

"All their farm trucks are automatic."

"Do you really think she would let me borrow a truck?"

"I'll broach the subject with Lady Elsmere tomorrow. I'm sure she'll say yes." I smiled, congratulating myself on fixing VeVe's problems. Lady Elsmere agreeing with my plan was as sure as gravy on a biscuit.

21

"**N**o!"

"What do you mean no? I gave that woman my word that you would let her borrow one of your farm trucks."

Lady Elsmere said, "I don't know her. She could get into a wreck and then sue me for a million dollars."

"That's nonsense."

"It is really?" June sneered. "Then you are not as worldly as you proclaim."

"This is a sweet woman who works as a secretary at the University of Kentucky making thirty-five thousand a year. By the time taxes are taken out, the woman barely has enough money to buy food for her cat and some chocolate bars for herself. You have so much. Why can't you help a sister in need?"

"You are always over here wanting things. Always yapping at my heels like some wayward mutt."

"June!" I gasped. I couldn't believe what she was saying to me. "You are not yourself." I stood up almost knocking over my teacup. "Is this your final word?"

"Yes."

I threw down my napkin. "I'll see myself out." I couldn't believe what had happened. June had never been in such a foul mood.

Charles was waiting near the kitchen door. "You look frightful."

I must have been more distressed than I realized because when telling Charles of my run-in with June I became incoherent.

Charles nodded sympathetically as he listened. Holding up his hand, he said, "Stop Josiah. I get the gist of your conversation. June's doctor put her on a new heart medication, and she's been an evil old bat since then. June's been so awful that Amelia threatened to quit as her caretaker, and you know Amelia loves June. This last incident with you proves the medication is causing a change in June's personality. I'm going to call her doctor immediately."

"Sounds like a plan, but I need an answer immediately, too."

"Tell me your issue again."

I related my need for a borrowed truck.

When I finished my tale of woe, Charles said, "You came at the right time. We have two trucks that we are going to trade in for newer models. Miss Veritas can borrow one and return it when she's finished, but she'll have to sign some papers first."

"What kind of papers?"

"June is not wrong about being sued. No good deed goes unpunished. I'll have June's lawyer draw up an agreement. Your friend can have the truck tomorrow, and it is an automatic transmission."

"It might be months before my friend can return it."

"That's okay. We've got plenty of vehicles. It's just cost-effective for us to trade work vehicles in after five years. I'll make sure our mechanic goes over the truck before we give it to your friend."

"Thank you so much, Charles. You don't know what this means."

"Things will get back to normal when June's medication is straightened out. Don't fret, Jo. This is only a temporary bump in the road."

"She upset me so."

"I could tell."

"I've never seen June so unreasonable. What am I going to do if that old witch goes senile?" It then struck me how much I love and depend upon June. I couldn't bear the thought of losing her.

Charles smiled. "You need a distraction. How's the investigation regarding Mr. Carpenter going?"

"Slow. No new leads as far as I know. The police are being awfully tight-lipped."

"It doesn't do any good for our fair city to have an unsolved murder of a tourist."

"No, it doesn't," I sighed, thoroughly worn out after my tussle with June. "Enough about me. What's going on with you, Charles?"

Delighted that he was asked about himself, Charles spouted, "I was asked to join Ferrina Landau's board to save retired Thoroughbreds. My first advice to the board was to partner with the Lexington Humane Society so we wouldn't be going after the same donors, but I don't think my suggestion was welcomed."

"There needs to be legislation on this issue."

"We need to educate the public first about this and illegal doping before we go after our legislators."

"You know best in these matters, Charles. Keep at it. Better yet, let Ferrina think your suggestions were her ideas. Butter her up. She wants to be the queen bee, so let her. If the ideas fail, she'll take the fall and not you."

Charles grinned. "And here I thought you were such a nice lady."

"You should have known better."

"One more thing before you take your leave. Ferrina is looking for a part-time secretary to help with this new venture. Mostly computer work at Ferrina's home. We don't want to spend money on an office when Ferrina has a space for office work. It will be for about ten hours a week that are pretty flexible but there will be weekend work. If you know of anyone reliable, let me know."

I just love it when gifts like this drop into my lap. "I know the perfect person for you, Charles. There absolutely couldn't be a better fit for this position."

Charles hesitated, but said, "If you say so, Josiah."

"Oh, I do, Charles. I do."

22

"How's it going?" I asked Franklin, sitting in the parlor at Wickliffe Manor.

"Well, I guess. Ferrina is a hard taskmaster. I don't think she knows what she's doing, but she does show passion for the issue of abandoned horses. I give suggestions when I think they're needed, but most of the time she ignores them. The main problem I'm having is that she is constantly changing her mind."

"How so?"

"Whom to contact. Do we do an email? Do we do a newsletter? Do we do Facebook? Do we do snail mail letters? There is no protocol set in place."

"Doesn't Ferrina know that you have helped with many fundraisers?"

"It doesn't seem to have an impact on her."

"What's going on in their house?"

"King took a fall after the kickoff party, so he is upstairs most of the time."

"I was at that party, and he did seem shaky on his feet. Anyone with him?"

"Chase is."

"No other caretaker?"

"I haven't seen one yet."

"Have you seen King?"

"No, but I hear him, knocking on the floor with his cane, and I see the kitchen help taking up his evening meal on a tray."

"Why don't they get a baby monitor?"

Franklin said, "They have a phone intercom system throughout the house. I hear Ferrina talking to King on it."

"Don't you think it odd with all their money Ferrina doesn't hire a nurse?"

"Maybe she has interviewed people while I'm not there. I've also seen brochures for assisted-living facilities."

"With all the square footage in that mansion, wouldn't it be more convenient to take care of King at home?"

"Maybe King requires more assistance than a nurse can provide at this stage, Josiah. He's a big man. Just to get him in and out of a shower would be a struggle, even with a male caretaker."

"That's why I have my big shower stall. When my time comes, just stick me in a wheelchair and push me in. I'll handle the rest myself."

Franklin scratched his nose. "You planned the Butterfly well. No steps. Extra large hallways and bathrooms. Easy to negotiate even if you're in a wheelchair."

"That's why it is referred to as a cradle-to-the-grave house."

"Hmm. Ferrina is installing a pneumatic elevator."

"That means King's condition is uncertain. They wouldn't be putting in a fifty thousand dollar elevator if King was being thrown on the scrap heap for good." I thought for a moment. "Were you able to do any nosing around?"

Franklin shook his head. "Ferrina keeps me pretty busy."

"You said Chase is helping take care of his father. Is there any talk about his going back to school?"

"I overheard Ferrina and Chase get into it about that very subject. Chase wants to stay home and help his father. He seems very devoted to King."

"Is Ferrina as devoted?"

"I think so, but in a different way."

"How so?" I asked.

"She recognizes King is on borrowed time and has faced it. Chase is in denial and thinks his father can recover."

"This sure paints a different picture of the Landau family. I always thought Ferrina married King for his money."

"I think Ferrina really loves King. If you're looking for medical or personal neglect with King, I don't think you'll find it. This new charity of Ferrina's is helping her prepare for King's eventual death. She will have an automatic support group, and something to occupy herself after King's demise."

"You talk as though you like them, Franklin."

"I don't like them, but I feel for them. Ferrina is a shrill, foolish woman and Chase is a stuck-up jerk. There is a malaise about the house. Perhaps the atmosphere would lighten up if Chase would go back to school. His presence causes a lot of drama. He's always second-guessing Ferrina which drives her crazy."

"Is Ellen Boudreaux over there much?"

"Ellen came a couple of times but she went upstairs in an attempt to visit King, and Chase laid down the law. Said King doesn't want any visitors and told her not to come back."

"Don't you find it odd that Chase doesn't want anyone to see his father?"

Franklin shrugged and shifted in his chair. "People are very self-conscious about infirmity. Maybe King doesn't want anyone to see him frail and bedridden. Maybe he just wants to rest. Visitors can take a lot out of an ill person."

"Can you be on the lookout for letters or a death certificate from an earlier wife?"

Franklin looked surprised. "King was married before? I didn't know that."

"I'm trying to verify his earlier marriages. June told me that her girlfriend had married King while she was in England, but King told me his first wife had died in a car accident."

"I don't mind eavesdropping, but I'm not going through someone's personal papers, Jo." Franklin took pity on my drooping expression. "Why don't you get online and check the state marriage register?"

"I did and I couldn't find any documentation of any marriage predating Ferrina."

Franklin thought for a moment and said, "Okay, he married out-of-state. Why not check Ancestry dot com or pay for a national background check? I do them all the time for potential employees. My office handles sensitive information, so we need to know that the employees are trustworthy. My boss doesn't trust the background checks people bring in, so I dig deeper. You'd be surprised what I find out about people."

"You do that and you're griping about looking for some old letters?"

"I can cover my tracks hacking a computer, but I could get caught rummaging through someone's desk."

"Then hack their computer, boy."

Franklin grinned. "I already have. There's nothing of interest on Ferrina's computer."

"Did you check her email?"

"Only baby boomers use email. Younger people text, Josiah."

"Excuse me for living. Did you check her phone then?"

"Not yet. She hangs on to that thing like it's an appendage."

"Find some way to get her away from it."

"Yes, swami."

"The others?"

"I've never seen Chase with a phone or a computer. He uses a landline to call out."

"A young man without a phone. Sounds odd to me. Chase's generation always has a phone on them."

"I agree."

"Find some way to check his room, Franklin. He's got to have a phone somewhere."

"No can do. Upstairs is off limits to me."

"So improvise. Jeez."

"Jeez, no way, Josiah. I'm not going to do any high risk snooping for you. I'll do some hacking and eavesdropping, but I draw the line at being called a thief which is what they will shout if they catch me upstairs. You forget I was accused of murder in the past. Now enough is enough."

I sighed and slumped in a sumptuous wingback chair. A slight breeze came through an opened window. It felt good. Though it was late autumn, it was unseasonably warm though it was forecasted that we were going to experience a cold November. "You're right. So sorry, Franklin." I decided to change the subject.

"When will Hunter be back?"

"He called this morning and asked me to meet his plane tomorrow. He sounded tired." Franklin offered to freshen up my iced tea, but I put my hand over my drink. "Will you be home Thanksgiving?"

"I plan on being home Thanksgiving, but Asa said something about the two of us going away the day after Christmas for a little R and R."

"I want to have Thanksgiving here at Wickliffe Manor. I'm inviting you and Asa and some other friends. I've already talked it over with Hunter. We're going to deck the place out. Have Christmas decorations already up. We're going to do nineteenth-century type stuff like bittersweet on the mantel, popcorn strings on the Christmas tree, a real pine garland winding up the staircase. The manor will smell like heaven, and I bought gobs of beeswax candles. Thanksgiving by candlelight. I can't wait."

I hesitated. "It sounds lovely."

"But?"

"I can't leave Matt and Emmeline alone on Thanksgiving. I'm sorry."

"How is Emmeline?"

"Growing like a weed. You should see her." I bit my lips. What a stupid thing to suggest.

Franklin emitted a barely audible sigh. "I would like to see her. Maybe I'll call Matt and invite him. He'll say no at first, but if you work on him, he might change his mind."

"That's very generous of you, Franklin. Are you sure you want to do that?"

"Matt and I made our peace a long time ago. I can't hold a grudge forever. I know it's over between Matt and me, but I want to keep my connection with Emmeline."

"Word on the street is you are dating."

Franklin chuckled. "Nothing serious. Basically going out with good friends for dinner and a movie."

"I see."

"Give me a few days before you mention Thanksgiving to Matt. I have to discuss this with Hunter first. He'll be resistant to the idea. He doesn't like Matt."

I stood up and called for Baby. "You let me know when."

"For sure. By the way, Jo, as to finding out information about King's wives, you have the perfect resource to nose around all you want." Franklin took the last sip of my drink. "Don't look at me blank like that. You know who I mean."

I slowly smiled. I sure did.

<h1 style="text-align:center">23</h1>

I called the number to an old fashioned answering service.

A woman with a Caribbean lilt to her voice answered, "Holden Caulfield's Answering Service. What is your message, please?"

I smiled at the reference to *Catcher In The Rye*. Asa loved her jokes. "Rosebud," I said.

"Thank you." The woman hung up.

Twenty minutes later, the phone rang.

I answered it.

"What's wrong, Mother?"

"Nothing that you can't fix, Asa," I replied, my fingers tapping impatiently on my couch cushion. Now I would get some solid answers instead of this bumbling investigation of mine.

24

"I don't know why you're angry, Hunter."

"I go away for a week and when I come back, I find my brother is employed by the very people involved in my last case."

"Franklin said he needed the money."

Hunter yelled, "It's unethical. I could be investigated myself over this. Josiah, you've gone too far this time. You don't seem to know when to quit. That morbid curiosity of yours has a cost to the people around you. You can't use your friends like chess pieces. This is not a game. I'm so mad, I could spit cotton."

"Then you're really not gonna like this. Franklin is thinking of inviting Matt to Thanksgiving."

"I know. He's already told me, but I don't want to talk about that right now. I gave Franklin orders to quit and hope the Landaus don't sue me."

"For what? They hired Franklin knowing his last name was Wickliffe."

"Did Franklin tell them he was related to me? No, I bet he didn't. That's the issue."

"I don't know what he told them."

Hunter sat down and put his head in his hands. "You're a wild card, you know. I never know what you're going to do or whom you're going to involve. You put yourself and others in danger all the time. What I don't understand is why people keep coming back for more of your crap."

I sat down beside Hunter. "It sounds like you are giving me my walking papers."

Hunter looked up. "Didn't it ever occur to you that if Franklin was discovered meddling, he would be in danger? Someone might hurt him or worse. I have only one brother, Jo."

"Before I even knew you existed, Franklin and I investigated cases together. He has worked with me on many murder cases. You talk about Franklin as though he was your best friend, but where were you when he was shot?"

"That's what I'm talking about. I don't want that to happen again."

"Yeah, he got shot, my dog got shot, and I got thrown off a cliff. I don't remember you being in the picture at all."

"That's because you were flown to Key West to recuperate leaving Franklin to deal with his wound and outrageous medical bills."

"Don't put this on me. You weren't there, Hunter. You were getting divorced in England for what—the third time? You know who was there for Franklin? Matt, that's who. It was Matt who was at the hospital. Matt who cared for Franklin during his recovery. Matt who paid Franklin's bills when he couldn't work. Matt who paid the rent on Franklin's apartment. Franklin said you called a few times, and that was it."

Hunter was nonplussed in the face of my tirade and continued without skipping a beat. "And then who else got shot because of you, Jo? Matt, that's who. And this time it didn't take a couple of months to recover. It was almost a full year, and he's still recovering. Have you taken a good look at Matt, Josiah? Really a good look."

I hung my head. "I know. I know. Matt looks— ravaged. I swear to you that I tried to get him to stay away. I begged Matt to live in town but he wouldn't. Don't you think I am filled with guilt every time I look at him?"

"You're dangerous, Josiah."

"Hunter, you can't blame me for all of this. I didn't kill a man and stash him in the back of my friend's car, nor am I responsible for a crazy cop who shot me and my friends either. The only thing I can do—the only thing that gives Franklin and me back our power is to go out and catch the bad guy. That's why Franklin went undercover to the Landau house. He wants his power back. That's why I can't let Shelby Carpenter's murder rest. It's personal. It's not a game with me. Can't you understand that?"

Hunter threw up his hands. "There's no talking with you. You're going to do what you want to do and the rest of the world be damned. I'm beginning to see."

"See what?"

"Nothing."

"Were you going to say you see why Brannon left me?" I couldn't believe Hunter was venturing down this road.

"Ellen might be a fool, but she's reasonable."

"When men say women are reasonable, they mean women who are malleable."

"Ah, here we go making this into a gender issue. Maybe Brannon left you because you were too irrational to live with."

I slapped Hunter's face and then recoiled at what I had done.

Hunter glared at me for a long time before he rose and quietly left. I didn't even hear the front door shut behind him.

What had I done?

What had I done?

25

I blew my nose into one of June's embroidered handkerchiefs. "I don't know what came over me. My behavior is inexcusable. I wouldn't blame Hunter if he never wanted to see me again."

Lady Elsmere handed me a teacup. "Take a sip of tea, dear. It will make you feel better."

"What am I going to do, June?"

"People act badly for a reason. Look at me. My new medication made me meaner than a caged panther."

"I'm not on any new medication. I can't use that as an excuse."

"I think finding Shelby Carpenter's body may have triggered something."

"Like what?" I asked, taking sips between pathetic little sobs.

"Josiah, you have been under tremendous strain for the past few years. Your husband left you for a younger woman. You lost your teaching position. You lost your savings. You were stalked. Saw your friends shot. Fell off a cliff. Almost lost your farm. Witnessed a murder/suicide at Matt's wedding and have been stumbling over dead bodies ever since. Your adrenaline system is in overdrive all the time."

"I don't understand what you're getting at."

"Humans either flee at the possibility of danger or they fight. You chose to fight but you haven't learned to turn off the impulse."

I burst into tears again and wailed, "You're condemning me, too! I *am* a bad person."

June thrust a slice of lemon pound cake at me. "No, I'm not. Stop balling at once. Here—eat this."

Sniffling, I managed to shove a piece of cake into my mouth. Yummy. It was so buttery, so lemony, and so light. This is what angel wings must taste like. Don't ask me where that thought came from.

June said, "I thought food would quiet you down."

"Who wants to cry when they can eat something like this?"

"Josiah, look at me."

I lifted my watery eyes. "Yes?"

"You shouldn't let Hunter get away. He's a good man. Besides that, he's educated, handsome, and is willing to put up with you."

"Am I that bad?"

"You're intimidating to men. You are intelligent, independent, resourceful, and brave—a force to be reckoned with. Those traits can be very daunting to men, even men advanced on the evolutionary scale like Hunter."

"I've never seen anyone as angry as Hunter. He was practically spitting at me."

"Oh, fiddlesticks. That's not true. You and Brannon used to have knockdown fights all the time—then play kissy face an hour later. Hunter probably regrets half the things he said before he was out the door."

"I don't know, June. You should have seen Hunter's expression after I slapped him."

"I guess the same expression you would have shown if he had hit you. Did it ever occur to you that Hunter was genuinely frightened for Franklin? Fear can make people angry."

I shook my head. "Never occurred to me. I didn't analyze what was going on. I just felt attacked."

"That's another thing, Jo. In all the time this havoc has been happening in your life, have you seen a therapist once?"

"I couldn't. When I had the time, I didn't have the money, and when I had the money, I didn't have the time."

"You are always running toward danger. Policemen, firemen, and secret agents do so because it is their job, but you run toward murderers as though it is your vocation."

"June, if you're trying to make a point, I'd wish you'd spit it out."

"Jo, I think you are suffering from battle fatigue."

"You mean PTSD."

"Call it what you will, but a professional should have a look inside your noodle. You've got to take better care of yourself. I would hate to outlive you."

"You can't deny that I have solved cases the police couldn't crack."

"I said you were smart."

"And I've saved lives."

"Point well taken, but look at what happened with Sandy Sloan—one of your best friends threatened to kill you with a shotgun. Who knows what would have happened if Darius hadn't come along, and she's not the only one to point a gun in your direction."

"In my defense, I came upon Sandy unexpectedly before realizing what she was doing. I didn't know she had already killed two people."

"You're not trained to see such things."

"The police didn't have a clue either."

"I'm not saying to stop sleuthing. You seem to have a knack for it."

"Then what are you grumbling about?"

"I just want you to be more careful. There—I've said my piece." June leaned back on the settee and took a sip of her tea.

"Slice me another piece of the pound cake, please."

"Are you going to think upon what I've said?"

"I'll study on it."

"Then you may have another slice of pound cake."

"Are you finished scolding me?" I asked.

"For the time being."

"Good. I would like to ask you a question then."

"Go ahead," June said, breaking the crust on a raspberry tart.

"You said your girlfriend married King Landau while you were in England."

"That's right."

"How did she die?"

"She's not dead. She's living in Miami with her daughter."

"Would you have her telephone number?" I looked at June with puppy dog eyes and whimpered.

"You are the living end. Will you go see someone if I do?"

"Yep."

June rang for Amelia who came into the library a few minutes later. "Amelia, get me my address book from my nightstand please."

Amelia scurried out of the room to retrieve the precious red leather-bound address book with names, phone numbers, and addresses from common laborers to duchesses.

When Amelia returned with the tome, June pointed to me. Amelia dropped the three pound book in my lap and returned to her afternoon tea with Bess in the kitchen.

"I have over sixty years of friends and acquaintances in that book. My life's experiences you might say."

"Whom do I look up?"

"Rockie Landau. You'll find her in the R's. Let me know what she says."

"I thought you didn't like my snooping."

"Yes, but I like gossip, and I'm a beast you must feed." June pointed a finger gnarled with arthritis at me. "Remember your promise. A phone number exchanged for a head doctor's visit."

I grimaced at the thought of seeing a shrink but a deal was a deal.

I wrote down Rockie Landau's number and hoped she was still alive.

Rockie Landau could break the case for me.

26

A woman answered on the third ring.

I asked, "Hello. Is this residence of Rockie Landau?"

"I go by the last name of Lancaster now. Who's calling, please?"

"My name is Josiah Reynolds. I'm a friend of Lady Elsmere."

"How is June? I haven't seen her in years."

"She's doing quite well for her age."

"I'm a few years younger but the last time I saw June, she looked fantastic."

"She still does, but she's now in a wheelchair occasionally."

"Ah, that's too bad."

"Miss Rockie, I was wondering if you could shed light on an issue for me."

"If I can."

"I hate to be impolite but this is a matter of importance. Do you know if King Landau was married before you?"

"That's odd. You are the second person to ask me that in a month."

"Who was the first person?"

"Oh, some man. Let me think. I think his name was Carter or Cartwright."

"Could his name have been Shelby Carpenter?"

"That's right. Said he was a reporter."

"What did you tell him, Miss Rockie?"

"I always assumed I was the first Mrs. Landau, but to be honest I don't rightly know. King never mentioned another wife to me. He talked about his childhood and high school, but he never said a word about his years from twenty to thirty. It's like they didn't exist."

"Wouldn't his relatives or neighbors have mentioned that he was married before? After all, people would have to have known of his wife's existence."

"King's people were dead by the time I married him, and he didn't have friends per se. He was a very private man."

"Did you ask about the missing years?"

"He would say there was nothing interesting to tell. Now that you ask about another wife, I once found a picture of a young woman in one of his shoeboxes. When I questioned him about it, he said it was his cousin and not to go through his things again. King divorced me shortly after I found the photo."

"You didn't ask for the divorce?"

"No, I told people that I did, but at this stage of life, why lie about it? King wanted out and badly. He went to Mexico and got a quickie. I never saw King again."

"I'm sorry."

"It was a long time ago. I wasn't madly in love with the man, so I wasn't devastated. I received a nice settlement, but the whole thing was odd. He said we weren't compatible, and he had met someone else, but he hadn't. It was just an excuse. All our friends said he wasn't seeing anyone as far as they could tell. Like I said—it was the strangest thing. He didn't remarry for a long time."

"Can you think of anything else, Miss Rockie?"

"Like I said before, King was a very private man. He would go off to his family farm and stay for days in a rundown house with no phone."

"You mean the horse farm he lives on now?"

"No. No. His family farm which lies in the knobs south of Berea. When we were married, King would put on airs that he came from early Lexington pioneer stock, but the truth is, his people are mountain folk, born and bred."

"I thought he was Bluegrass aristocracy."

"It's all a lie, pure and simple. The man had brains and guts, but no lineage."

"How do you know this? You said he didn't talk about his past."

"When I found the woman's picture, I also found

King's high school yearbook. It told me all I needed to know."

"Did you ask him about the yearbook?"

"Not after he got so upset with me finding the photograph. I didn't have the courage. I had struck a tender nerve for sure."

I paused trying to think.

"Why are you and Mr. Carpenter asking these questions?"

"I believe Mr. Carpenter was murdered for asking questions."

Rockie said, "Then you better be careful, my dear, if you are making the same inquiries as the departed Mr. Carpenter."

Having the last word, Rockie Landau hung up.

27

I had to run into the library to pay some late fees, so my plan was to duck in quickly and get out before Diane Voss spotted me. I didn't want any trouble, but who should turn around and wait on me at the counter?

Diane Voss.

Oh, snap!

"I need to pay fees for these books. Keep the change," I said, throwing a ten-dollar bill down on the counter and scurrying out the door.

"Mrs. Reynolds. Mrs. Reynolds!"

I kept heading for my car.

"Please don't make me run after you."

I stopped and turned. It was okay by me if Diane wanted to cause an unpleasant scene in the parking lot. "Ms. Voss."

She broke off her pursuit in front of me, breathing heavily. "Let me catch my breath."

"I didn't mean to upset you, Ms. Voss. I didn't

know you were working at the counter."

"May I speak with you for a moment, Mrs. Reynolds? I am sorry I was so freaked out when we talked before. I should have realized you were sleuthing. That's what you do, right?"

"In a manner of speaking."

Diane surveyed the parking lot of onlookers. "Can we talk in your car?"

"About what?"

"I think there is something you should know."

"I'm game." I showed Diane to my Prius and we both got in.

"What do you want to tell me, Ms. Voss?"

"This stays between us."

"I can't make any promises."

Diane paused for a moment.

I urged her to speak. "Obviously, there is something on your mind, Ms. Voss. I'm not an attorney or a priest, but I'll be as discreet as I can."

"You are the second person to question me about the Landaus. The first one was Shelby Carpenter, so you can see how asking questions about me dating Chase freaked me out. I mean the Carpenter man was murdered. At first, I thought you might be working for the Landaus."

"Working how?"

"I didn't drop Chase. I was paid off by his mother to end the relationship."

My eyebrows rose and my stomach got that wonderful tingly feeling when I'm on to a good clue.

"Chase and I were serious. I genuinely cared for him. We even talked about marriage after we both graduated, but when Ferrina got wind of our plans, she would have none of it. She came to me and offered me fifty thousand dollars if I would leave Chase."

"Which you took."

"I was drowning in debt with student loans, and my mother had been diagnosed with cancer. I needed the money."

"Does Chase know?"

"I told him why I couldn't see him for a while, but I never thought our separation would be forever. The Landaus have money coming out their whazoos. I was desperate, but Chase didn't understand. He has no conception of what it is like to be poor."

"Is that why he flunked out of school?"

"Yes. He did it because he was angry with Ferrina."

"Ferrina's emerald necklace has some of the smaller gems replaced with paste. Almost looks like the real thing. Was Chase flinching emeralds from his mother's necklace to pay his gambling debts?"

"He intended to make an engagement ring for me."

I flinched a bit. It didn't make sense to me that a bride would want an engagement ring made from stolen gems, especially if they belonged to her mother-in-law. Her story didn't ring quite true, but I assumed she was trying to make Chase sound noble. Chase was probably using the money from the sale of the gems on drugs and gambling. "Do you know where those stones are now?"

Diane shook her head.

"Do you stay in contact with Chase?"

Diane shook her head. "I've tried calling and texting, but he won't respond."

"What was Carpenter asking you about?"

"General questions. Were the Landaus a happy family? Why did I break up with Chase? Did old man Landau have any violent tendencies? Had I ever met his former wives? There wasn't much I could tell him."

"Wait a minute. Carpenter asked you about Landau's former wife?"

"He asked about *wives*. He was very emphatic about it."

"In the plural?"

"Yes."

"What did you tell him?"

Diane pursed her lips. "I didn't even know Mr. Landau had been married before Ferrina."

I patted Diane's arm and said sympathetically. "Okay. Okay. Anything else?"

"This may sound awful, but I don't regret taking the money. My family is debt free for the first time in twenty years, and my mother got the medical help she needed. She's in remission now. Sometimes sacrifices have to be made for the greater good. I lost Chase but my mother got a few more years. That's a good trade, isn't it?"

I wanted to kiss Diane's forehead. "It's a very good trade. Now that King Landau is very ill, I'm sure Chase understands your decision."

Diane's eyes brightened, and she gave me a smile before heading back to the library.

I watched Diane until she disappeared through the doors of the library.

I would not trouble that dear girl again.

28

"I think I found a motive for murder," Asa told me in a late night phone call.

I sat up in bed and asked breathlessly, "What?" I could feel a tingle running up my spine.

"King Landau was married at the age of eighteen to a woman named Dixie Orr, who was twenty-two at the time."

"A May-December match for mountain folk," I said sarcastically.

"Not only that," Asa said, "but Dixie was King's Sunday school teacher."

"You sound disapproving, Asa. People married young back then, and couples often met at church. The dating pool in the mountains was small because getting around was difficult. Midwives from the Frontier Nursing Service were still going into the mountains on horseback and mules in the late sixties."

"If you say so."

"Gosh, you're spoiled. What else did you find out?"

"The trail ends after a year."

"What do you mean the trail ends?"

"No more Dixie."

"Huh?"

"There is no record of Dixie Orr Landau after the first year of her marriage. Poof. She's doesn't exist anymore. No bank records, driver's license, employment records, Social Security payouts, medical records—nothing. The woman disappeared off the face of the earth."

"That fits in with the story King told me about his wife dying in a car crash."

"There is no paper trail for King or his wife even owning a car at the time."

"She could have been a passenger in another person's car. Another explanation is that people in the mountains often barter. Maybe someone gave them a car for a wedding gift?"

"There are no tax records or registration for a car under the Landau name, and I mean any Landau until long after King Landau had left the area."

"Now how would you know that? Those old records wouldn't be on the computer."

"Because I sent someone down to Kentucky to search the records by hand."

"I wish you hadn't done that. I just wanted a quick look-see."

"You're welcome, Mom."

"It's not that I'm not grateful. I don't have the money to pay you back."

"Call it a pre-Christmas gift. Franklin called me and said you and Hunter had a huge dust-up."

"The little snitch."

"Mother!"

"I said 'snitch.'"

"Well?" Asa pressed.

"Hunter's mad at me for involving Franklin in my investigation."

"Is that what we're calling your snooping now? I'm surprised the police haven't knocked on your door and warned you off. I understand Detective Drake is very territorial."

"I am, too."

"Have you and Hunter made up?"

"We haven't spoken since the argument."

"That's going to make Thanksgiving awkward since we're going to Wickliffe Manor."

"I'm not going. I can't leave Matt and Emmeline alone on Thanksgiving."

"It's all arranged. Franklin and I have been texting each other. Matt and Emmeline are going, but you have to pick up Lady Elsmere and bring her."

"What about you?"

"I'll be flying in on Thursday morning. I'll meet you at Wickliffe Manor."

"Has this been okayed by Hunter?"

"Don't know. Don't care. Hunter will get with the plan once he sees he's outnumbered."

Not wanting to discuss Hunter anymore, I segued back to King Landau. "Anything else about King and his first wife? You said you found a motive for murder. I haven't heard it yet."

"Oh, yeah. The most important tidbits. My guy found their marriage certificate but no death certificate for Dixie Orr, and we checked every state surrounding Kentucky. Now get this. We dug up a newspaper article in a county newspaper about a family complaining about a missing family member and posting a reward regarding her whereabouts. Guess who it was."

"Dixie Orr Landau," I said.

"Correctomundo. In the article, King stated Dixie had run off with a fancy man."

"Heard that excuse before."

"I've sent you a copy of the article along with Dixie's birth and marriage certificate. That's all I can do at this point."

"Do you know what happened to King after the newspaper article was published?"

"He went out west to make his fortune just like Horace Greeley recommended, only to come back to Kentucky in his late thirties."

"Thanks, Asa. I'll take it from here."

"Mom. You and I both know what happened. I've read the reports on Shelby Carpenter's murder. Be careful. Even as an old, sick man, King Landau has sharp teeth. I wish you would let this matter drop."

But I couldn't.

I don't know why, but I couldn't.

29

After Asa's call, I went to check on the animals. An early snow threatened, which was strange because we usually didn't have much snow until January and February. "What do you think, Baby? Are we going to get a white Thanksgiving?"

Ignoring me, Baby ran ahead to the horse barn. Most of the horses were still out in the pastures, but I had put my horse, Morning Glory, up in a stall because I wanted to wash and groom her again. I didn't like her dirty. "Hey, Glory. I have some peppermints for you," I called out, but when I got to her stall, she was gone.

My heart dropped.

A note was hanging on Glory's tack by the stall door.

Josiah,

I have Morning Glory. Don't worry about her. See you at Thanksgiving. Miss you. Hunter.

Hunter took back my horse! Calm down. Calm

down. He said he was going to have Morning Glory retrained after I fell off, so maybe that's what he was doing with her. Jumping Jehoshaphat! He could have given me a heads up. Guess Hunter was still angry. Hope he gets over it by Thanksgiving, so we could share a pleasant meal. I was ready to kill, oops, I mean kiss and makeup. Freudian slip there.

He did say he missed me in the note.

I missed him, too. There. I said it. Here's another thing—I hoped we could repair the rift between us. Hunter was a lovely man, and I did understand his point of view.

I was just going to have to lie better in the future, so Hunter wouldn't worry because he would bust a gut if he knew what I was up to.

Yeah, lying. That's the ticket.

30

Frost hung in the air as Franklin and I stepped out of my car, grabbing some shovels. Hazel greeted us with her German Shepherd which was a cadaver search dog. "I can't thank you enough, Hazel."

"This makes it square between us," Hazel stated. Hazel was an old friend of mine who trained cadaver and rescue canines. She had worked with me recently to find a woman who my neighbor, Sandy Sloan, had murdered. Sandy no longer receives a Christmas card from me, but Hazel does.

"It does."

"Where do you want me to start?" Hazel asked, looking at the late nineteenth century home whose day had come and gone. Most of the windows were broken or missing, and the front porch sagged into the front yard. Even if the porch had been attached, we couldn't push through the weeds to get inside.

Hazel looked about and took note of the *No Trespassing* and *No Hunting* signs. "I take it we are on this land illegally."

Franklin answered, glancing around like a frightened doe. "Kind of."

"Then let's get our story straight. We were hiking and didn't know we were trespassing," Hazel suggested.

"Got it," I said.

Franklin nodded. He held a shovel, identical to mine, in a white-knuckled grip.

"Franklin, are you up for this?" I asked. "You can wait in the car."

"If we are confronted by Bigfoot or a panther, you are on your own. I'll leave you in the dust. Just so you'll know."

"Noted," I replied, grinning, but I think Franklin was serious.

"Where do you want to start?" Hazel asked.

"Where do you suggest?"

Hazel gave her dog a treat. "Let's start with the outbuildings first and then the outlying land. I don't want to go into the house unless I need to."

"Okay," I said, turning toward Franklin. "You ready?"

"Let 'er rip," he said.

Hazel gave a command to the German Shepherd, and he took off pulling Hazel with him.

Franklin and I pushed through the briars and weeds as best we could. I was glad I was wearing my heavy duty coveralls, gloves, boots, and a wool hat that came over my ears. My get-up protected me from ticks and snakes, but it was heavy, making me lurch and stumble as I tried to follow. After a half-hour, I couldn't pursue Hazel any longer. I had to rest.

"Jo, I think it's best you go back to the car and wait," Franklin said as I leaned into a huge pin oak tree, trying to catch my breath.

"I'm sorry, Franklin, but I think you're right. I'm in the way."

"Do you know the way back?"

"Sure. I'll be fine. Here—take my water. There's more in the car."

Franklin took the bottle and tucked it into his small knapsack. "Blow your whistle if you need help," he said, referring to a bright red whistle around my neck. "Is your phone on, though I don't know if we can get any reception out here."

"Go on. I'll be fine. Just need to catch my breath."

Giving me one last concerned look, Franklin said, "Blow that whistle if you need us to start back."

"Stop nagging, Franklin. You're losing the trail."

Franklin ran off in search of Hazel, leaving me panting by the majestic oak tree whose maroon and orange leaves were drifting to the ground in a gentle wind. I slid down the tree and looked up at its massive branches. "Hello, tree. May I rest here a bit?" I paused for a minute, listening to the forest sounds. "Yes, you say. Thank you very much." I needed to shut my eyes before I made my way back to the car.

Just for a moment, I thought.

31

I jerked awake. What had hit me? Reaching up, I knocked an acorn off my head only to look up and spy a chattering squirrel scolding me for disturbing her home. She dropped another acorn on me. I must have been snoring. Quickly looking at my watch, I saw that an hour had passed. Straining, I listened quietly but didn't hear Franklin, Hazel, or the occasional barking of the dog. I wondered if they had headed back to the vehicles and were now looking for me or perhaps they had found something, and Franklin was digging it up.

Either way, I needed to vamoose. I flipped over on my knees and tried to pull myself up using the tree as support. My knees were not having it. Okay. That was not working. Another acorn hit my head. "Hey, stop that," I yelled at the squirrel, who scampered further up the tree trunk. I could still hear her chattering angrily. "I'm trying to leave. Give me a moment."

I reached over and grabbed the shovel, thrust it into the ground, and used it as leverage to pull myself up.

Did it. Now I needed to find my car. A breeze blew through permitting the oak's branches to shift. The sun peeped through the moving leaves for just a second or two when something shiny in the earth caught my attention. "What is that?" I murmured. I carefully dug it up and reached down to retrieve it from the loamy soil, bringing it close to examine. It was a very old metallic button in the shape of a heart. "Can't be Civil War. A woman's button I would say."

Stepping back, I surveyed the area where I had been lying. There was a slight depression in the ground. I put the button in my pocket before making another swipe in the dirt and then another. Two more buttons and a scrap of cloth with a pattern of flowers emerged. Then I found a hammer. I kept on digging. Uncovered a bone. Looked like a finger bone, but could be a chicken bone for all I knew. I dug near the base of the oak tree searching until my shovel skimmed something hard.

Lowering myself gently to the ground, I scraped the dirt away with my hands until I found the top of a yellowish dome. It was cracked and a small piece of it was missing, leaving a tiny hole. I was quiet for a long time listening to the breeze and the call of the birds before I reburied the buttons, the cloth of a woman's dress, and most importantly, the hammer.

The squirrel chattered again.

"I know. I know. You were trying to tell me. I misunderstood at first, but I found her—thanks to you, sister."

The squirrel ran up to its nest and disappeared.

Dragging the shovel, I made my way back to the cars where Franklin and Hazel soon joined me, bedraggled and exhausted. We drank water and ate some peanut butter crackers before getting into our vehicles and making tracks out of there.

On the way home, I told Franklin what I had found. He stopped at a big-box store where I purchased a prepaid phone and called the state police. Afterward, I threw the SIM card out on the highway.

Then Franklin and I waited to see something in the newspaper.

We didn't have to wait long.

32

I was at the farmers' market selling honey. It was a slow Saturday as it was cold and gloomy. I was hopping around trying to keep warm when Detective Kelly stopped by.

"How's my favorite honey lady?" he asked.

"Long time no see."

"Been busy, Josiah."

"How's everything at home?"

"Good. Real good. Back on track." Kelly was referring to his relationship with his wife after his affair with my daughter. I didn't condone it. I'm just telling you.

"Glad to hear it, Kelly."

"Almost forgot. Brought you some hot chocolate." He handed me a Styrofoam cup.

"You are a dear." I took a sip. "Nice and hot. For that you may take some honey home. This is goldenrod honey. It's dark and thick, but not overly sweet."

"No thanks. I had some last year. I thought it tasted bitter."

"It can. I'm not too fond of it myself, but people clamor for it. They say this honey helps with their allergies."

When a customer came to the table to purchase honey, Kelly stepped back. "See what I mean?" I said, handing the customer her change. "I thank you and the bees thank you."

When the customer left, Kelly asked, "Can I come behind the table? I need to speak with you."

"Sure. Come on. I have a heater under the table. It will keep our toes warm while the rest of us freeze."

Kelly stood next to me while I sold another bottle of honey.

I said, "You're my good luck charm. Can you stay until I sell out?"

"Did you read the paper yesterday?" Kelly asked.

"I did."

"And?"

"And what?"

"A woman's body was found on King Landau's old family farm buried under an oak tree. Her skull showed shows of blunt force trauma and a hammer was found buried with her."

"The paper said the woman was identified as Dixie Landau, King's first wife."

"That's right, Jo."

"How did they identify her?"

"Her purse was thrown into the grave along with

other personal items."

"No DNA?"

"No one to compare her with. All her close kinfolk are dead. She's been in the ground for decades."

"What does King Landau say?"

"Said he doesn't know who the woman is. Anybody could have buried her on his property. Said he hadn't lived there for over sixty years."

"And yet he kept the farm."

"Does he say what happened to Dixie?"

"Says she ran away with a man."

"Did King divorce Dixie?"

"He says he has a copy of the decree but can't remember where, so we are looking into it."

"He went to Mexico for a quickie divorce with his second wife."

"We might not be able to prove or disprove his claim about this divorce if he got his divorce out of the US sixty years ago. A good defense lawyer could plant reasonable doubt about the ID of the remains because we don't have dental records or DNA."

"Any fingerprints on the hammer?"

"Too degraded."

"Then Detective, you don't have a case. Even if you proved beyond a shadow of a doubt that the woman was Dixie Landau, you can't prove King killed her."

"Any suggestions?" Kelly asked.

"If I were a detective, I would call his second wife,

Rockie Landau, and see if she has something to tell you."

"Does she?"

"She might mention a photograph of a woman in a shoebox. If that picture still exists, it might have a name on the back. If it doesn't, you can still have a forensic artist do a facial reconstruction of the features from the skull and compare it to the picture."

"Nothing will come of it. King Landau is dying and in a hospice."

"Yeah, but you might tie King to the murder of Shelby Carpenter. I think Carpenter was doing a piece on King and asking too many questions. He might have stumbled onto Dixie and King's marriage certificate and wanted to know what happened to the first Mrs. Landau, not knowing he was stirring up a hornets' nest."

"You think King hired a professional hit on him?"

"I think someone in that family either killed Carpenter himself or knows who did. Do you really think Ferrina cares about anyone knowing she was a call girl?"

Kelly's eyes narrowed. "How do you know that?"

Ignoring his last question, I said, "But she would care if Carpenter was getting close to finding out there was a body buried on the old homestead."

"She's down at headquarters right now being grilled by Drake."

"Great minds think alike."

Another customer came up and purchased several bottles of honey. "Gonna be here next week, Josiah?"

"This is my last Saturday until next year. It's getting too cold."

"Then give me four more bottles. The honey's got to last me through winter."

"Here you go. See you next year. Remember—you can freeze honey, but you shouldn't put it in the fridge."

"Thanks, Josiah. Have a great winter."

"You bet."

I put the cash in my pocket. "My money is on King. I doubt Ferrina or Chase even knew King had been married to a Dixie Orr."

"How do you know her maiden name?"

"Don't ask. Don't tell."

"I think Chase did it. He felt his father was being threatened by Shelby Carpenter or perhaps overheard Carpenter attempting to blackmail King, so he follows Carpenter and seeing an opportunity, shoots him."

"It takes someone very cold blooded to shoot someone on a street in the middle of a city. That person has to be cool headed and collected. I don't see Chase being such a person. He's too emotional."

"There's no hard evidence connecting King to either case. It's all circumstantial."

"Looks like you are going to have two unsolved

cases on your hands."

"Darn it. I hate that. I would really like to crack this case wide open."

"Unless you get a deathbed confession, I think it's unlikely." I took another sip of my hot chocolate.

Kelly looked at his watch. "I've got to go. My shift starts soon. One more thing before I go."

"Yes?"

"A woman called in the tip about the body to the State Police. You wouldn't know anything about that, would you?"

"I've learned my lesson about getting involved in police matters. Glad you stopped by and thanks again for the hot chocolate."

"Always, Jo." Kelly walked away with a little jaunt in his step. I couldn't help but think of what might have been if Asa hadn't left him after high school. He would have been a wonderful son-in-law.

A customer stepped up to my table, which shook me out of my reverie.

Life was what it was, and there was nothing I could do to change it.

Or could I?

33

I told the nurse I was an old friend and wanted to say goodbye. She told me to be brief, saying it was doubtful King Landau could hear me.

I promised her I would only take a moment.

I walked into the room.

King was attached to a tangle of tubes and wires, but he was breathing on his own. There was the ever-present catheter bag tied to the side of the bed, and the TV was showing a game show with the sound off. Everywhere there were flowers and get-well cards, but there was no getting well for this man. This was the end of the line for King Landau.

I pulled a chair close to the bed and pressed into King's thin, gnarled hand the dirty heart-shaped metal button off Dixie's dress she had worn on the day she was murdered. I closed his fingers over it. "King," I whispered. "I know you can hear me. Feel that button. It's Dixie's button, King—from the dress she was wearing on the day you murdered her with a hammer.

What did Dixie do wrong that day, King? Burn the meatloaf? Not starch your shirts stiff enough? Tell you she was leaving? Everybody knows, King—the secret you kept hidden for over sixty years is out in the open. Everybody knows you are a wife killer and that you had Shelby Carpenter killed as well. Tell the truth. Don't take it to the grave with you."

King stirred and struggled to open his eyelids, which fluttered like a butterfly's wings in flight.

"I knew you could hear me."

"She had it coming," he rasped. "She had it coming."

"And Shelby Carpenter?"

"No."

"You're dying. What does it matter now? Get it off your chest, man."

"No."

The nurse stuck her head in the door. "You'd better go, ma'am. His blood pressure is going through the roof."

I glanced at the monitor and saw King's heart was racing. "He's all yours," I said before walking out the door and never looking back, though I wondered if King was still clutching the little heart-shaped button that a woman had lovingly sewn on a feed sack dress over six decades ago. I wish I had kept it.

34

"June, get in the car," I barked, exasperated. "We're going to be late."

"Give me a minute, Miss Priss," June groused. "It takes a moment to get these old legs working."

Amelia handed me a bag. "This has all her medications and personal items that she'll need."

"Check," I said, tossing the bag in the back alongside the black walnut cake, double chocolate brownies, blackberry cobbler, lemon tarts, and a tomato pie Bess had made for June to take to Wickliffe Manor.

"Let me help, Lady Elsmere," Matt said, handing Emmeline to me. He provided a strong arm for June to balance herself while she struggled to get from the wheelchair inside the car.

"I can walk," June insisted. "I just can't walk far."

"I can pick you up," Matt offered.

"Oh, would you?" June said, batting her eyelashes.

I shook my head. "Come on, June. Quit flirting and get in the car. Charles is waiting for Amelia. The

Dupuys have their own Thanksgiving to get to."

Matt settled June in the car, strapping her in the front passenger seat.

Amelia poked her head inside and gave June a quick peck on the cheek. "Call me if you need me."

"Tell that to Josiah. If I need help, I doubt she'll let me use a phone."

"Don't worry, Amelia. June will be fine. Won't you, you old goat?" I said, handing Emmeline back to Matt, who put her in a car seat in the back.

June shot back, "Old, ill-tempered women are bats. Old, ill-tempered men are goats."

Strapped in by her father, Emmeline was fussy, so Matt gave her a bottle.

"I hope you put Benadryl in that baby formula," I murmured.

Matt complained, "You have no patience, Jo." He turned to Amelia. "I'll keep a close watch on all three gals and text you every so often so you won't worry. We'll be fine. Josiah's a very good driver when she has passengers. She'll make an effort not to hit the side of a barn."

Starting the car I said, "Heard that. Everyone got their seatbelts on?"

No one answered. June was fiddling with her purse and Matt was tending to Emmeline, who had thrown her bottle on the car floor.

Seeing that everyone was secure, I honked the horn

for everyone to wave goodbye to Amelia, whose face relaxed into one of relief.

"Amelia's glad to see the back of us," I commented.

"I can't wait to eat. I'm drooling over the black walnut cake," June said. "It's one of my favorites."

Matt said, "I think I'll have some warm blackberry cobbler. I hope the Wickliffes have vanilla ice cream on hand."

"Have you been to Wickliffe Manor, Matt?" I asked.

"Just a few times. Franklin showed me around before I left for California."

"You should see it now. Very spiffy. Hunter and Franklin have done a lot of work to it."

"I look forward to it. I brought a bottle of bourbon for Hunter and champagne for Franklin as a thank-you for inviting Emmeline and me. I very much appreciate it."

"I'm sure they'll enjoy the libations," I replied, looking at Matt in the rearview mirror. I could tell he was nervous.

"Jo, could you drive a little slower around these curves? I don't want Emmeline to toss her cookies on her new dress. I'd like to keep her clean until we get there at least," Matt said, cleaning off Emmeline's mouth with a wipe and arranging the bow in her hair.

Emmeline stuck her fist in her mouth and gurgled.

I slowed down. "I don't think I've ever seen a white Thanksgiving. We must have two inches of snow.

Thank goodness the snow plows got out early this morning."

"Where's Asa?" June asked.

"She told me she would meet us at Wickliffe Manor but she didn't give me a time," I answered.

June asked, "Is she bringing that man with her?"

"You mean her Russian sidekick, Boris—or is he Ukrainian? I can never remember."

"I thought he was Georgian," Matt said.

I replied, "I don't know. She didn't mention him."

"Why isn't Baby with us? He goes everywhere with you," June said.

"Yeah. Where's Baby?" Matt asked.

"Hunter came and got him last night. We didn't have room for him in the car today."

"Watch it, Jo. Looks like there's black ice on the road," Matt cautioned.

I slowed down and put on my emergency blinkers so the car behind me knew something was amiss. The car slid a bit but I maneuvered it out of danger. The car behind me wasn't so lucky and slid off the road.

We pulled over on the shoulder and stopped.

Matt got out and ran over to the unlucky car. He talked for a moment with the driver and then got behind the car to push.

I unbuckled my seat belt and hurried over to the disabled car, careful not to slip on the ice. I doubted that I was much help, but Matt and I pushed the vehicle back onto the road. I think Matt did most of the work. The couple waved a "thank you" as they ventured down the road to their own Thanksgiving.

Matt and I scampered back to the warmth of my car feeling pretty good about ourselves and the world. I pulled back onto the road without incident and took my time traveling to Wickliffe Manor.

After all, I had precious cargo in my car.

35

The massive iron gates to Wickliffe Manor were open with each gate gaily displaying a festive green bow with oversized red ball ornaments and ribbons.

"Looks like Franklin is ready for Christmas, too," Matt said.

"He said he was going to have the house all decked out," I said.

June cried, "WATCH OUT!"

I slammed on the brakes causing the car to skid to a complete stop. "Everyone okay? I'm so sorry. I didn't see it around the curve."

In the middle of the road stood my beloved American Paint, Morning Glory harnessed to a bright red sleigh complete with gold trim and jingle bells.

Hunter and Baby jumped down from the sleigh and ran over to us.

Looking sheepish, Hunter said, "I'm sorry, folks. We were trying to meet you at the gate, but no harm done that I can see."

"What is this?" I asked.

"This is your new toy. I didn't think you would ride again after your fall, so I had Glory trained to pull a wagon."

Matt and Emmeline shot out of the car to explore the sleigh. "She's a beauty, Hunter," Matt said, running his hands over the sleigh's trim.

I got out and went over to Morning Glory. She neighed, tossing her head. "Hello, old girl. Miss me? I see that you've got a new gig." Turning to Hunter, I asked, "Where did you get the sleigh?"

"Borrowed it from a friend of mine. We can use it for as long as we like. Glory's been practicing since yesterday." He patted Glory's neck and looked at me expectantly. His brown eyes looked as bright and shiny as two new pennies.

"I'm amazed. The sleigh is a beauty, Hunter."

"Want a ride in it?"

I stepped forward and gave Hunter a tight hug. "Very much so."

"Matt, can you drive Lady Elsmere to the house? I want to take my best girl for a spin."

"Sure thing, but can Emmeline and I have a ride in the sleigh, too."

"Be delighted to. Wait for me on the portico. After I drop off Josiah, I'll take you two for a spin."

"Great. Thanks, Hunter." Matt got into my car and drove toward Wickliffe Manor as Baby chased it.

"How do I get into this contraption?"

"Put your hands on these handles and pull yourself up."

"Give me a boost."

Hunter put his hands on my fanny and pushed me up, allowing me to climb in somewhat competently if not gracefully. He clambered in after I got settled. "Surprised?"

"It's a lovely surprise, Hunter."

"Look, Jo. It's snowing."

Laughing, I stuck out my tongue to catch a snowflake. The air was icy and fresh with snow covering the tree limbs.

Hunter huddled close and tucked a blanket around my legs.

"You get under too," I said, lifting the blanket so he could scoot under.

"Look," I said, pointing ahead.

Baby ran toward us and jumped in the back, heavily panting, but looking rather pleased with himself.

"He must have taken a bite out of my bumper," I mused.

Seeing Baby was secure, Hunter took the reins and gave a little twitch with them, saying, "Walk."

Morning Glory strained to pull the sleigh. It jerked forward and stopped.

"Give her a minute," Hunter said. "This is new to her."

"Maybe you're giving her the wrong command," I suggested. I dreaded the thought of walking the long driveway to Wickliffe Manor.

"Let's try this again. Morning Glory—walk!" Hunter said more forcefully.

Morning Glory whinnied and moved forward, pulling the sleigh on a nice even clip. Other than the clomping of hooves and the jingling of the bells on the sleigh, all was silent. The falling snow enveloping us was magical.

I broke out into song. "Jingle bells, jingle bells. Jingle all the way."

Hunter joined in—"Oh, what fun it is to ride in a one-horse open sleigh!" He finished Jingle Bells until he had to negotiate a bend, giving Glory commands, "Come left. Come left. Walk now."

"Hunter, I didn't know you had such a wonderful tenor voice."

"You should hear me in the shower. I'm a show-stopper."

I snuggled closer and hoped I remembered this to the end of my days. The snowy drive to Wickliffe Manor in a sleigh with my honey bun was one of the most beautiful events in my life. It's always the small moments that stand out in one's life.

"Are we okay?" I asked.

"Do you want us to be okay?"

"I do."

"I hear a 'but.'"

"I'm no prize."

"Neither am I."

"I'm not going to change, Hunter. I like solving mysteries. I seem to have a knack for it."

"I don't deny that." Hunter pulled me closer. "I flew off the handle because I was frightened for both you and Franklin."

"What you do is dangerous, too."

"It's different."

"Why? Because you're a man?"

Hunter grinned. "It's hard to bypass those ideas drilled in when a child. Men protect women and younger brothers. It's written on my DNA code."

"I think it's a wonderful quality to have, Hunter, but I don't need any protection right now. Can I let you know when I do?"

The sleigh hit a bump as Morning Glory veered off the road.

"Right now, I need your help in getting this horse in the right direction. She's heading for the barn. Morning Glory, come right. Come right," Hunter said as he and I tugged on the right rein.

My little pony managed the correction smoothly. I was very proud of her.

Once Hunter got Morning Glory back on track, he said, "I'll never let you down, Jo. I'll be there when you need me."

Was that a snowflake melting on my cheek or was it a tear? I quickly wiped it away. "Let's have the most special Thanksgiving we've ever experienced, Hunter. I know I've got a lot to be thankful for. I'm very grateful for all my blessings."

Hunter looked at me with those bedroom eyes of his and said, "Me, too."

The sleigh jolted to a stop as Morning Glory rested in front of Wickliffe Manor's portico where Franklin waited with hot toddies on a silver tray.

Was this a postcard Thanksgiving or what!

36

Asa and Boris arrived at Wickliffe Manor before Hunter finished carving the turkey.

Boris brought a jar of homemade borsht from his homeland as a gift.

Franklin quipped, "How did you manage to smuggle this out?"

From the startled expression on Boris' face, it was obvious he had smuggled it out, which delighted Franklin all the more.

Overcoming an anxious patois at first, Matt and Franklin fell into an easy parlance as though they had never been apart. Franklin brought his old high chair down from the attic and placed it between himself and Matt, so they could take turns dealing with the Emmeline. She had been denied a nap and over stimulated by a ride in the sleigh. You know what that means. Emmeline was a brat, but still every time she burped, Franklin snapped a picture.

"Franklin, leave that baby alone," I admonished.

"Why is she even at the adult table?" June asked.

Hunter chuckled, "Where are we to put her, Lady Elsmere? In the kitchen by herself?"

"If you insist."

"As soon as we get some food into her, she'll fall asleep," Matt reassured.

I spooned out a heap of mashed potatoes and filled her sippy cup with formula. "Try this, Matt."

Of course, Emmeline refused to eat, so Matt lifted her from the high chair and went to rock her in the old fashioned cane chair in Hunter's office.

"Shall we wait for Matt?" Asa asked.

"The food will get cold. Let's proceed," Hunter suggested.

We all bowed our heads and said a silent prayer until Franklin said, "Amen."

After unfolding my napkin, I helped June. As heaping bowls of steaming food came my way, I put small helpings of greasy green beans, milk skillet corn, sautéed heirloom beets, mashed potatoes, macaroni and cheese, acorn squash casserole, fried okra, turkey, gravy, butter rolls, cornbread, and honey butter onto my plate and then on June's before passing the bowls to my right.

"Goodness! I don't know if I can eat all this," June exclaimed.

"Just eat what you want, June," I said.

Franklin teased, "I'm sure whatever is left on your

plate, Josiah will scarf it up."

"I thought that's what the dog was for," June groused, her feet resting on Baby's back who was lying under the table.

"Ha ha. Very funny. I don't like to see food go to waste, that's all," I protested.

A phone rang one time.

Everyone looked up.

"It's not mine," Asa said as everyone stared at her.

"I think it's the landline," Hunter said, listening for another ring. Hearing none, he said, "Seems like they've changed their minds. Eat up, everyone. Eat up."

Matt popped his head around the dining room's pocket door. "Excuse me. Hunter, there's a call for you. It's the police."

Hunter threw down his napkin. "Couldn't this wait until tomorrow?"

"Can you take it in the kitchen? Emmeline's sleeping on your office couch."

"No problem." Hunter looked around the table while rising from his chair. "Folks, I'll be back in a jiffy."

Matt moved Emmeline's high chair to a corner and took his place beside Franklin, who passed bowls and platters of food to him. Matt piled food on his plate until it overflowed. Noticing everyone's curious expression, Matt said, "I don't get a chance to eat such wonderfully prepared food without a baby sticking her dirty fingers in my hair, so I'm going to take advantage while I can. After I feed Emmeline and put her to bed, I'm usually standing over the sink eating a microwave dinner from a cardboard box."

"Oh, you poor dear," Asa retorted in a mocking tone.

Matt grimaced at her before he slopped another helping of milk corn on his plate.

June said, "You're going to make yourself sick."

"Wanna bet?" Matt said.

Hunter came back into the room and sat down.

"Who was it, brother dear?" Franklin asked, filling Hunter's wine glass.

"Just work. Nothing interesting."

Franklin and I glanced at each other. We both knew Hunter well enough to know he was fibbing.

Hunter lifted his glass of wine and said, "This is what life is all about. Good friends, family, and good food. Salute."

We all lifted our glasses and cried, "Happy Thanksgiving!"

37

After dinner when everyone was napping, I caught Hunter sneaking out with his briefcase. "Where are you going?"

"That was Norbet Drake calling. He wants me to come down to the police station."

"On Thanksgiving!"

"You gotta move when the evidence is in and things are hot in this business. Don't tell everyone I've left. I'll be back as soon as I can."

"Hunter, it's beastly out there. You shouldn't be driving in weather like this."

"Sorry, Jo. I'm under contract. I've got to jump when the police say."

"I'm going with you then. We'll take Asa's Jeep. It will do better in the snow."

"Don't, Jo."

"Everyone's sound asleep, so they can wake up and partake in another run at the vittles. Matt can use my car to get home, but he'll probably wait until morning.

The roads look awfully bad, Hunter. Can't you go tomorrow?"

Hunter shook his head while pulling on his gloves. "Drake wants to make an arrest today, and he needs me there to observe a suspect during the police interrogation."

Seeing that I couldn't talk Hunter out of going to the police station, I hurriedly wrote a note and left it on the side table by the front door. Ransacking Asa's purse, I found her car keys. "Let's go."

"Won't Asa be angry that we took her vehicle?"

"Assuredly, but it's too small for everyone to hitch a ride back to Lexington, so this is the best use of her car. Come on. Let's go."

Hunter opened the front door and I stepped onto the portico covered with three inches of snow. "It's really coming down. Let me help you, Josiah. The steps look slippery."

I was not about to get all huffy about Hunter acting as though I was an invalid. Hey, wait. I practically am. The bracing cold made my left leg feel stiff causing me to hang onto the handrail before stepping down. When I had negotiated the last step, I breathed a sigh of relief. Hunter helped me into the Jeep. "Hunter, do you think Glory is okay?"

"I put her in the barn where she's got plenty of hay and water."

"It's so cold."

"I put a blanket on her. Glory's fine. What about your animals?"

"There are five Chilean interns on June's farm taking care of the horses today and tomorrow. They'll check on my animals, too. I hope they remember to break the ice if the water freezes."

"Let's worry about us. I want to get to the police station before dark. We don't have much time."

Hunter eased the vehicle down the driveway as I checked the radio for weather reports. What should have been a thirty-minute drive took us over an hour, but we finally made it to the police station in downtown Lexington, which looked like a frozen ghost town. Cheerful holiday lights and lighted decorations shone through the falling snow. Everywhere the holiday spirit was evident with Kwanzaa, Hanukkah, and Christmas symbols adorning Main Street, but the thoroughfare seemed eerily quiet. No parked cars. No people walking. No stores open. No noise. To be honest, it was creepy.

Hunter parked in the No Parking zone right in front of the police station. I got out and followed him inside where Detective Kelly was waiting. Surprised to see me, Kelly gave me the once over, but Hunter said, "Josiah is working with me on this case."

"Drake is not going to like this," Kelly said. "Josiah's not trained."

"The police hire outside their venue all the time—

anthropologists and entomologists, to name a few. I bring a unique perspective. After all, I am an art history professor."

Kelly shot back, "You *were* a professor."

"In which interrogation room is he?" Hunter asked, referring to Drake.

"B," Kelly answered.

"Follow me. I know the way," I said, "since they have me down here every week it seems."

Hunter and I went into the observation room of Room B and found that Drake had already started his questioning of Chase Landau perched on the hot seat. I took a seat next to Hunter who was already making notes on a legal pad.

Drake said, "Let me express my condolences on the death of your father."

So the old geezer had finally thrown in the towel.

Chase replied, "Save it. I want to go on record that searching our house and forcing me to come down here on the day of my father's death, not to mention Thanksgiving, is a despicable and disgusting trick."

"Noted," Drake said, "but I want it noted that I'm missing Thanksgiving with my family as well."

"Then let's do this tomorrow. My mother needs me."

Drake ignored Chase's last statement and plowed on. "Were you aware a body was buried on property owned by your father, King Landau?"

"I was not aware of any dead body as I was not even aware my family owned that land."

"It was the Landau's family farm. You claim you had never gone there. Didn't know it existed?" Drake asked.

"My father never talked about the past and never mentioned this property. The fact that a woman was found buried on his farm is as shocking to him as it was to me, Detective. Let me ask one thing here. How do you know that the woman didn't die of natural causes and was buried there because her family didn't have to money to have a proper funeral?"

Drake pulled out a picture of a hammer and laid it before Chase. "Have you ever seen this hammer before?"

Chase glanced at the picture. "No."

"Take a good look. Did your father own a hammer like this?"

"I do not use hand tools nor did my father. We have staff who make repairs on our properties, including our personal home. Perhaps you should ask one of our workers."

"Did your father ever mention a woman named Dixie Orr Landau?"

"No."

"Are you sure?"

"Is that the woman's name buried on the farm?"

"Yes."

"Never heard of her." Chase folded his arms defiantly.

Drake pulled out another photograph. "Then how do you explain the fact we found a button from the dead woman's dress in your bedroom?"

Chase glanced at the photo and his face drained of color. He seemed to lose some of his swagger and refused to meet Drake's stare.

"Buttons like this one in the photograph were found on a dress Miss Dixie was wearing on the day of her demise." Drake tapped on the photo. "All the buttons from her dress have been accounted except for one. Yet we find the one missing button in your room."

"Probably picked it up at a flea market or something."

"You collect women's buttons, do you?"

Chase drank from his glass of water. "You can't prove the button from my room is a button from the same dress."

"But we can. The button is rare. It's made of tin. We couldn't find one for sale on the Internet, but we did talk to several button collectors. They had never seen one like it before. It was their opinion that these buttons were handmade from tin cans. They would be considered folk art today."

"So?"

"There's also the dirt on the button. We are having

the dirt tested to see if it matches the dirt from the gravesite."

"No comment."

"Were you aware the burial site of Dixie Landau had been disturbed recently?"

I squirmed in my seat, but never let out a peep.

"No."

"Did your father disturb the gravesite? Was it his intention to move the body after Shelby Carpenter began asking questions about Dixie Landau?"

"You're suggesting my elderly father with Parkinson's disease was trying to unearth a dead woman and then rebury her elsewhere? You must be daft, man."

"Did you help your father dig up Miss Dixie?"

Chase slammed both palms flat on the table. "No. No. No."

"Do you have knowledge that your father acted alone or hired someone else to dig up Dixie Landau's grave?"

"No, you stupid man."

"How did you come to have one of the heart-shaped buttons in your possession?"

"I don't remember. Must have picked it up at a flea market, like I said." Chase leaned forward until his face was inches away from Drake's. "Maybe one of your flunky cops planted it?"

Drake snorted derisively. "Did your father give you the button, Chase?"

"No. I've already told you. I don't know a thing about that button."

"Did your father confess the murder of Dixie Landau to you?" Drake asked.

"No."

"I found it odd that you haven't asked who Dixie Landau was?"

Chase's face grew hot. "No comment."

"Then I don't have to explain that Dixie Orr Landau was your father's first wife."

Chase looked away.

"Did he tell you about her?"

"Didn't even know she existed."

"Did you know your father had married a second woman before he married your mother?"

"Yes. They got a divorce long before he met my mother."

"Did your mother ever mention a Dixie Landau?"

Chase shook his head wearily. "NO!"

"Are you surprised to discover your father had a wife whom you knew nothing about?"

"My father was a private man."

"Did he mention why he killed Miss Dixie?"

"Nice try, Detective. My father did not kill this Dixie person. You have not shown me how this woman died. How do you know she didn't die a natural death?"

Drake slid out another photograph. "Perhaps this hole in her skull will enlighten you. Someone had to be awfully angry to strike a woman from behind with a hammer."

Chase picked up the photograph and flung it back at Drake.

Undeterred, Drake asked, "What do you know of this woman's murder?"

Chase shouted, "NOTHING!"

"Did you kill or have any knowledge about the death of Shelby Carpenter?"

Chase looked stunned.

So Drake had connected Shelby Carpenter's death with the Landaus. About time.

"Did you, your father, or another person carry out the execution of Shelby Carpenter?"

"Don't answer that, Chase," boomed a voice from the doorway. A man burst into the room with a briefcase—his casual attire signaling he had also been called away from a Thanksgiving dinner. Uh oh, the lawyer had arrived and he looked mighty irritated. Fuming, he hissed, "Are you going to arrest my client?"

Drake leaned back in his chair. "We would like for him to take a lie detector test."

"Our answer is no." He turned to Chase. "Did you drink out of the glass?"

"Yes."

The lawyer pulled out his wallet and threw a five-dollar bill on the table before picking up the glass. "We're going to take this glass. I'm sure you weren't trying to trick my client into giving away his DNA and fingerprints by giving him water. Let's go, Chase. Your mother is waiting in the lobby."

Chase stood, gave Drake a self-satisfied smile, and strode from the room with the lawyer.

Drake glanced into the two-way mirror we were sitting behind before tidying up his files and leaving the room.

"What do you think, Hunter?" I asked.

"Chase is definitely hiding something."

"I think his father gave him that button and confessed before he died."

"What makes you think King had the button in his possession?" Hunter asked.

"Umm. Just a hunch."

"It's obvious Chase adored his father. He could have had knowledge of Dixie and tried to move her body. That's why the body was disturbed."

"Perhaps his father confessed, and Chase went to see if it was true or the ramblings of a disoriented man. Found the body, and then covered it back up." No use pointing in my direction. Oh, crap. That would make Chase an accessory after the fact. Oh, crap. That makes me an accessory after the fact. No, wait. I called it in. Whew. That gets me off the hook.

"Possibly, but why not tell Drake if that were the case?"

"He didn't want his father's name tarnished.

"Which is a motive for killing Shelby Carpenter."

"Chase kill Carpenter? No way. The boy's a marshmallow." I just keep getting this kid deeper and deeper in doo doo. I felt Chase had nothing to do with Shelby Carpenter's murder. Of course, I've been wrong before about people.

Hunter put his legal pad away. "Chase knows more than he is saying. I think he's very much involved in this somehow." Taking out his laptop, he typed from his notes and sent an email. "Done. We can leave now. Drake's got my notes. I'll just stick my head in his door before we leave. You can wait in the car. Warm it up, please." Hunter gave me a beseeching look.

I knew the real reason he wanted to get rid of me was so he could face Drake's wrath alone. I took the keys and made my way out into the cold. Turning the engine on, I listened to Christmas music until Hunter made his way out and into the Jeep.

"Well, how did it go?" I asked.

"Drake said something about your personal anatomy being caught in the wringer."

I instinctively clutched my breasts. "Ouch."

"I'm too tired to drive all the way back to Wickliffe Manor. Can we bunk at your house tonight?"

"Sounds like a plan. I have two pumpkin pies waiting for us."

"Hey. Things are looking up."

"It's a good thing I forgot them. Now we have

something to snack on."

"It's not Thanksgiving without pumpkin pie," Hunter said.

A lonely snowplow pushed past us.

I mused, "We are not the only ones working on Thanksgiving."

"Poor schmuck."

"Let's head on out, Hunter. I can make a nice fire, and we can snuggle in front of the fireplace, eating ourselves sick with pumpkin pie."

"Got whipped cream?"

"The heaviest."

"You are a treasure." Hunter followed the snowplow out of town and onto Tates Creek Road.

It wasn't long but before we were home—safe and sound curled up in each other's arms.

38

Ferrina asked Ellen Boudreaux to handle the gathering after the funeral, but Ellen, still smarting from Chase throwing her out of the Landau's house, refused. What a peach!

So Ferrina asked Franklin to help so the staff could attend King's funeral, and I volunteered to help Franklin. See how that works. I had more investigating to do and what better time to do it than while everyone was attending King's funeral.

Yes, it is unethical, but if sleuths always acted ethically, we would never solve any crimes. See. It's a conundrum. We act unethically to catch unethical people.

Franklin and I entered the kitchen to find a list of errands we were to do and food to prepare. The cook had already made items for the wake. All we had to do was set out the dishes and beverages on the buffet table.

One of the errands listed was to check all of the

bathrooms and make sure there was adequate toilet paper.

Franklin looked at me, saying, "You get that gig. I'm going to heat up the meatballs."

No problem. It would allow me to roam the house. I passed through the dining room to the main foyer. I checked the hallway bathroom, which was spotless with its gleaming marble floors, sparkling sink, and luxurious hand towels. I had to think for a moment how many bathrooms were on the first floor. Ah, there was King's bathroom in his study. Great. Maybe his desk would be unlocked, and I could go through its contents.

I pitty-pattered down the hallway gleefully only to gasp when I stepped into King's study. The French doors were flung open with glass from a busted frame on the floor. Books were scattered about the room, and King's treasured mementos were in tatters. Paintings had been ripped from their places on the walls with the backings cut from the frames. King's portrait torn from the wall exposed a safe.

Shocked at the damage to the room, I stepped deeper inside not thinking. Oh boy! I shouldn't have taken that extra step.

"Don't move or I'll blow your brains out," came a raspy voice from behind.

Yes, it was a corny and trite thing to say, but it certainly caught my attention, especially when a gun was pressed to my temple. "Don't turn around."

"Wouldn't think of it."

"Who are you?"

"I just came to help prepare for the wake."

"Who else is here?"

"No one. I'm by myself."

"You're lying. I heard you talking to someone."

"Then why are you still here?"

The stranger pressed the muzzle of the gun into my flesh. "I will have no compunction in killing you, lady."

"I believe you." This is when I kind of wet my panties.

"Who else is here?"

"Two other people came to help. They're probably outside bringing food in from the catering truck. If you leave by the French doors, they won't even see you."

"Do you have the combination to the safe?"

"Why would I have the combination? I'm just a caterer who will be missed soon if you don't let me go."

"Let's go see your friends."

"Did you look through the desk? The combination is probably written down somewhere."

"I did."

"Did you look under the drawers? Sometimes elderly people write on the underside of wooden drawers."

The man grabbed my neck and dragged me over to the desk. "Not a bad idea. You look for me."

I ignored the impulse to turn around and see the

man's face, knowing that if I did he would kill me for sure. I pulled out each drawer and turned it upside down. On the third drawer, I found faint marks on the underside. Do I know people or what!

The man instructed, "Sit in the chair and face the other wall. Read me the numbers."

Shielding my eyes and bowing my head, I sat in King's chair and read the marks recorded in pencil. I heard the man head over to the safe and try the numbers.

"It's not working."

"No need to get excited." I bent over closer to read the numbers. "The markings are faint. Try this."

Grunting and cussing, the man worked the combination while I pondered if I could make it to the door and down the hallway before the intruder caught up with me. I decided it was too much of a chance. With my bum leg, I wouldn't be fast enough. There was a sterling letter opener on the desk. I surreptitiously palmed it while I felt around with my feet. I came upon the phone, which he had thrown onto the floor. It had an intercom connection with the kitchen. Slowly taking off my shoes, I pressed on the receiver with one big toe and pressed the kitchen button with the other big toe. *Please, please, Franklin. Pick up.* "Did you find what you were looking for?" I asked in a loud voice.

"What's it to you?" the man replied.

I heard items being dropped on the floor. "Look,

the Landau family and guests will be arriving very soon. In fact, I think I hear cars in the driveway now. You can go out this door. I haven't seen your face. You have no reason to hurt me. You can make a clean getaway."

The man jerked me out of the chair, dragging me toward the dining room.

"Stop! What are you doing? You got what you want. Just go."

The man's grip was like iron, and I couldn't pull away. Talk about feeling like a rag doll being jerked around. The only thing I could do was to drop to the floor like a dead weight, screaming, "RUN, FRANK-LIN!"

I looked up and saw the man was startled but he collected himself in a split second. It was time enough to point the gun down at me. Unlike Shelby Carpenter, I saw the gun coming toward me, so I did the only thing I could. I reached up and grabbed the man's privates. Boy, did I squeeze and twist like there was no tomorrow because if he didn't drop that gun, there would be no tomorrow for me.

The man gasped and sputtered in shock, trying to smack my hands away. Furious, he pointed the gun at me again.

Oh, God! Oh, God! Don't let me die like this. Shrieking like a banshee, I took my fist and punched him in the you-know-what as the coup de grace. The gunman dropped the gun and sank to the floor in agony.

Franklin ran from the kitchen with an iron skillet in his hand ready to do battle. Seeing the man writhing in pain on the dining room floor, Franklin kicked the gun away out of the man's reach and ran back in the kitchen, returning with a roll of Duck tape. "Are you all right?"

"I'll live," I said, grinning, "but I think he might need medical attention. I might have squished some things rather important to him."

"Where he's going, he won't need them. Who is he?"

The attacker groaned.

"He's the man King Landau hired to murder Shelby Carpenter. Isn't that right?" I asked as I wrapped tape around the man's feet while Franklin taped the man's hands still clutching his "personal life."

"What's he doing here?"

"I would bet he hadn't been paid by King. Let's check the man's pockets, shall we?"

Franklin and I rummaged through the killer's pockets and wallet as he unleashed a vile stream of curses prompting Franklin to tape the man's mouth shut. "Well, mister, we're just going to have to plug up that potty mouth of yours. No one calls me that and gets away with it," Franklin said.

We found several bundles of cash he had taken from the safe and a wallet with six different ID's.

"Ooh, he's been a busy lad," I said, looking at each of the names on the driver's licenses. As much as we wanted to go through everything, we had to stop as the police stormed the house with guns drawn.

Apparently, our gunman had tripped the security alarm.

Franklin and I raised our hands.

"Hi, guys. What took you so long?" Franklin asked, smiling.

The police were not amused.

39

The gunman was charged with assault with a deadly weapon, carrying a weapon without a permit, breaking and entering, burglary, and terroristic threatening. However, he came up clean in CODIS, and DNA searches proved futile. His moniker was Mark Goodson, if you can believe that was his real name.

The cops ran a ballistics test on his gun, but it wasn't a match for the slug, which had killed Shelby Carpenter. Without any proof he had killed Shelby Carpenter, the police couldn't hold him on a murder charge. Because Goodson had no priors, his bail was set at a fifty thousand dollars and you know who paid it? Take a wild guess—the Landau family.

That guy was out of jail within forty-eight hours and disappeared before the ink was dry on the check Ferrina had written. Not really. That's a metaphor. More like the time it took Ferrina to swipe her credit card.

The police were doggone sure King Landau had

killed his wife, Dixie Orr Landau, but couldn't prove it, nor could they conjure a reason for it. They suspected King had hired Mark Goodson to assassinate Shelby Carpenter, who was doing a piece on King and had stumbled upon the fact that King had a first wife whose very existence had been a closely guarded secret. Carpenter's questions caused King to fear the blogger was getting too close to the truth and had him done in.

Chase had either figured out his father's duplicity or had received a confession from King. He left school to help cover up his father's crimes and protect him, but the police couldn't prove that either.

Hunter and I protested when Drake consigned the murders of Dixie Landau and Shelby Carpenter to the cold case files.

Frustrated at how things had turned out, Drake argued, "Give me some evidence I can run with, and I'll open these cases back up. I'm just as sick about this as you are, but the law's the law. I have no witnesses. I have no fingerprints. I have no DNA. In other words, I have nothing. I must have hard evidence. Not supposition."

Drake was right. Nothing could be done. King Landau had gotten away with murder—twice. I wondered what King had said when he met his maker. The conversation couldn't have gone well, I think.

The only bright spot was that the Landaus bought VeVe a brand new car and paid her fifty thousand dollars not to speak of the incident outside a court of law again. Shaneika Mary Todd helped her with the transaction.

They offered the same to me, but I refused. Mark Goodson had shoved a gun to my head, terrorizing me. I wanted justice, not a bribe.

One thing is to be sure—if it hadn't been for me the police would still be twiddling their thumbs.

It is great to be queen.

40

June decided to invite fifty of her "closest" friends to a champagne breakfast on Christmas day. Guests were seated at one long table in the ballroom, and a buffet was laden with her favorite Christmas foods, including piggy pudding and spotted dick. In anticipation of the repast I had dreamt of chocolate walnut fudge and sugar cookies shaped like stars and Santas. Piggy pudding and spotted dick were really low on my list of goodies, but hey, it wasn't my gig. All I can say is that June must have been in a Charles Dickens phase. I was fine with it as long as she kept to her new medication regimen and didn't turn into Scrooge.

A collection of extravagantly decorated Christmas trees bordered the ballroom, all with eye-popping decorations. One tree was more outrageous than the next. We are talking glitter, twinkling lights, and enough tinsel to supply a New York ticker tape parade.

Matt and Franklin fawned over Emmeline, who was overawed by the elaborate decor. Asa gabbed with

Amelia while a bored-looking Boris nursed a mug of eggnog that he had generously spiked with bourbon. Charles and Mrs. Dupuy hummed along with the Christmas music looking quite content. Mrs. Dupuy must have gotten good news from the doctors.

Much to my surprise, Baby had received his own engraved invitation. He went from person to person begging for treats and nudging for scratches behind the ears. Some people enjoyed my big canine and slipped him a nibble or two. Others shooed him away, disgusted at the strings of drool dripping from his chin and his ruined eye.

And me?

I was pulled into a corner by Hunter.

"I wanted to give this to you when we were alone, but it looks like that's not going to happen for a while—so here goes." Hunter presented me with a small blue box.

"Tiffany's?"

"Your Holly Golightly dress at the benefit inspired me."

"This box is too pretty to open."

"Just open it, Josiah."

"Don't rush me." I put the bow in my pocket and opened the blue box. Inside was a gold bracelet with a slip of paper. I gave Hunter a curious look. Pulling out the paper, I slowly read the note.

Written in cursive was, "I love you!"

It had been a long time since any man had said he loved me.

"Well?"

"Give me a minute, will ya?"

"Aren't you going to say you love me, too?"

"No."

"Why not?"

"Because I would like to say it without you coaching me, Hunter."

"But you do."

"Maybe."

"Merry Christmas, Josiah," Hunter said, pulling me close and kissing my cheek.

I hugged him back and gave him a quick peck on the lips. "Merry Christmas, Hunter."

Speaking of Charles Dickens—"A Merry Christmas to us all. God bless us, everyone!"

The End.

Like to receive special offers?
Feel free to sign up for my newsletter at
www.abigailkeam.com.

Did you like Death By Deceit?
Please leave a review.
Thank you.

Other Books By Abigail Keam

Mona Moon Mysteries

Princess Maura Tales

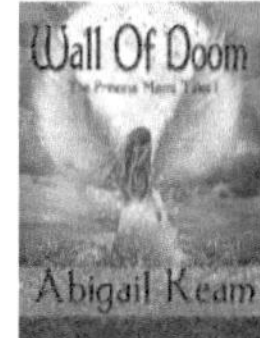    

Josiah Reynolds Mysteries

Last Chance For Love Series

CHECK OUT THE
JOSIAH REYNOLDS MYSTERIES!

"Abigail Keam writes with vision and understanding."
Midwest Book Review

"We are introduced to a cast of characters and a storyline that, like honey, is sweet and delicious."
Linda Hinchcliff, Chevy Chase Magazine

"Ms. Keam writes such that readers want to know more of Josiah's life and the ending will not disappoint their need to know."
Readers' Favorite

The Last Chance For Love Series

After her divorce, Eva Hanover leaves New York City and heads for the Florida Keys. She buys a rundown motel in the seediest part of Key Largo, intending to restore it to its mid-century glory. As Eva refurbishes the motel, the magic of love returns and guests find a second chance for love.

About The Author

Hello, my friend. I hope you enjoyed *Death By Deceit*. I have such fun writing about Josiah and her quirky friends. If you like to read in other genres, I also write *The Princess Maura Tales*, a high fantasy series and *The Last Chance For Love Series*, a happily-ever-after sweet romance series. I would love to hear from you.

abigailshoney@windstream.net

If you like *Death By Deceit*, please leave a review. and tell your friends about me.

www.abigailkeam.com
Newsletter: abigailkeam.com/newsletter
Twitter: @AbigailKeam
Facebook: facebook.com/AbigailKeam
Instagram: instagram.com/abigailkeam
Pinterest: pinterest.com/abigailkeam